ReShonda Tate Billingsley

*Her bestselling novels of family and
faith have been hailed as*

"Emotionally charged . . . not easily forgotten."

—*Romantic Times*

"Steamy, sassy, sexy."

—*Ebony*

"Compelling, heartfelt."

—*Booklist*

"Full of palpable joy, grief, and soulful characters."

—*The Jacksonville Free Press*

"Poignant and captivating, humorous and heart-wrenching."

—*The Mississippi Link*

Don't miss these wonderful novels

THE PERFECT MISTRESS

"Billingsley is skilled at making flawed characters sympathetic,
even as they meet painful justice."

—*Booklist*

"... I advise you to hold on to your books or e-readers. You are in for one heck of a ride."

—*Romance in Color*

MAMA'S BOY

One of Library Journal's best books of 2015

"This outstanding story that handles every mother's nightmare from multiple views while addressing one of society's deepest controversies. The end was like watching a cliffhanger that one did not see coming!"

—*RT Book Reviews*

WHAT'S DONE IN THE DARK

"An entertaining book with suspense, drama, and a little humor . . . The twists and turns will have readers rushing to turn the pages."

—*Authors & Readers Book Corner*

THE SECRET SHE KEPT

A TV ONE original movie

"Entertaining and riveting . . . Heartfelt and realistic . . . A must-read."

—AAM Book Club

SAY AMEN, AGAIN

Winner of the NAACP Image Award for Outstanding Literary Work

"Heartfelt . . . A fast-paced story filled with vivid characters."

—*Publishers Weekly*

EVERYBODY SAY AMEN

A **USA Today** *Top Ten Summer Sizzler!*

"A fun, redemptive book, packed with colorful characters, drama, and scandal."

—RT Book Reviews

LET THE CHURCH SAY AMEN

#1 **Essence** *magazine bestseller* • *One of* **Library Journal's** *Best Christian Books* • *A BET original movie!*

"Billingsley infuses her text with just the right dose of humor to balance the novel's serious events."

—Library Journal (starred review)

"Her community of very human saints will win readers over with their humor and verve."

—Booklist

A GOOD MAN IS HARD TO FIND

"Billingsley's engaging voice will keep readers turning the pages and savoring each scandalous revelation."

—Publishers Weekly (starred review)

HOLY ROLLERS

"Sensational . . . [Billingsley] makes you fall in love with these characters."

—RT Book Reviews

THE DEVIL IS A LIE

"A romantic page-turner dipped in heavenly goodness."

—Romantic Times (4½ stars)

SEEKING
SARAH

ReShonda Tate Billingsley

GALLERY BOOKS

New York   London   Toronto   Sydney   New Delhi

G

Gallery Books
An Imprint of Simon & Schuster, Inc.
1230 Avenue of the Americas
New York, NY 10020

First Gallery Books trade paperback edition August 2017

GALLERY BOOKS and colophon are registered trademarks of Simon & Schuster, Inc.

For information about special discounts for bulk purchases, please contact Simon & Schuster Special Sales at 1-866-506-1949 or business@simonandschuster.com.

The Simon & Schuster Speakers Bureau can bring authors to your live event. For more information or to book an event, contact the Simon & Schuster Speakers Bureau at 1-866-248-3049 or visit our website at www.simonspeakers.com.

Interior design by Bryden Spevak

Manufactured in the United States of America

10 9 8 7 6 5 4 3 2 1

Library of Congress Cataloging-in-Publication Data is available.

ISBN 978-1-5011-5662-5
ISBN 978-1-5011-5664-9 (ebook)

SEEKING
SARAH

CHAPTER 1

Yes! Yes, I'll marry you!

The words swirled around in my head, dancing with excitement at the prospect of marrying the man I love. The perfect proposal. The perfect man. All the ingredients for a dream come true.

But for some reason, while the words were vibrant in my mind, they wouldn't come out of my mouth.

Good grief, woman, just say yes!

That little voice that had planned my proposal and subsequent wedding when I was only ten years old and marrying my imaginary boyfriend was in full what-the-hell-is-wrong-with-you mode.

Just say yes.

Still nothing.

I don't know what was wrong with me. If you asked most women to draft a list of the qualities they wanted in their dream man, Trent Grant would probably meet 99 percent of the requirements on their list. Trent had dabbled in modeling in college and despite an offer from a New York modeling agency, he had opted to go into the Navy instead. He'd served eight years as a sergeant and returned to Raleigh as one of the most sought-after bachelors in town. And he wanted a life with me. And I wanted a life with him. Only my mouth wouldn't open to say yes.

I knew my fear was based on the fact that Trent wanted forever and I'd learned long ago that forever didn't exist. And committing to a lifetime was only setting myself up for heartbreak, something I'd vowed I would never let happen again.

"Wow, soooo, is that a no?" Trent asked, as he knelt in front of me. Just the thought seemed to crush his spirit. His thousand-watt smile had morphed into a frown. "You don't want to be Mrs. Grant?"

The piercing gaze of all of our family and friends reminded me that we weren't alone. There had to be twenty-five people in the private dining room at Ruth's Chris Steak House, all of them waiting on my answer. The room had grown deathly silent. The only noise was the slow trickle of the April showers beating down on the roof. The smiles that just seconds ago were beaming now bore hints of nervousness.

I snapped my attention back to the man in front of me. I did want marriage. I did want happily ever after. I just didn't believe that such a thing was possible.

Still, I managed a smile and said, "O-of course. Of course, I'll marry you."

A relieved applause erupted in the room as Trent slid the three-carat ring onto my finger. It was beautiful and I hated that this experience had been marred by my hesitation. If Trent was upset by my delayed response, he didn't let on. Instead, he stood, then pulled me into him with a force that told everyone just how happy he was.

Trent wrapped his muscular arms tighter around me. Over his shoulder, I saw my father beaming with pride. I thought we'd gathered at this dinner party to celebrate Trent being awarded the North Carolina Man of the Year by the League of Distinguished Men. This proposal was a complete surprise. We'd talked about getting married—one day. I had no idea that day would happen so soon. But apparently Trent and my cousin April had been working overtime to plan a surprise engagement party.

For Trent, we might as well have been the only two people in the room. He lifted my chin and the love I saw in his eyes made any reservations I might have been feeling evaporate instantly.

"I swear, Brooke, I want to spend a lifetime making you the happiest woman in the world," he whispered.

I smiled, but didn't reply. Don't get me wrong, I was happy. Very. I loved Trent. But as I fingered the two rings on my necklace, I remembered the two loves I'd lost, and fear suffocated my excitement.

As Trent basked in congratulatory greetings, I continued fingering the rings—my mother's wedding ring, which my dad had presented to me on my sixteenth birthday, and an engagement ring from Jared, the only other man I'd ever loved. I wore both faithfully on a small gold chain around my neck.

Several people came over to congratulate me: my friends, my coworkers from the public-relations agency where I worked as a publicist for celebrity clients, and a few of Trent's family members.

My father approached us, the pride on his face his stamp of approval. "You know I'm expecting you to take good care of my baby girl," he said to Trent.

I couldn't help but marvel at how handsome my father was. His silver hair was a stark contrast to his smooth, dark skin. It was hard to believe he hadn't remarried after all these years, but it wasn't for a lack of offers. Like me, he had never completely healed from my mother's death.

"Awww, Mr. Hayes, you don't have to worry," Trent said, taking my hand until we were fully intertwined. "I promise you, she's in good hands."

"I know that, son." My dad patted Trent on his back. "And you come from good stock, so I know you understand that marriage is supposed to be forever."

I forced a smile at my father. He was always talking about how life had robbed him of his forever. My mother had died when I was seven, so my father harbored some bitterness that kept him from finding love again. I guess losing her had tainted me, too. Because growing up, while I dreamed of my wedding, I hadn't been too psyched about marriage. Then my heart betrayed me and let Jared in.

We'd met at freshman orientation at North Carolina A&T University. Though we'd dated all four years of college, I wasn't one of those girls who were planning their happily-ever-afters. Then, on my twenty-second birthday, I'd let Jared convince me in forever. I agreed to marry him. And three weeks before our wedding, Jared was killed by a carjacker.

The therapist that I'd started seeing after Jared's death eventually helped me to heal my heart, but it hadn't destroyed the belief that the people you love most always leave.

Trent's mother tapped her fork against her champagne glass, snapping my attention to the front of the room, where she was standing.

"May I have your attention please?" The chatter that filled

the air slowly trickled down as we turned our attention to the poised, bubbly, petite woman at the front of the room. "For those of you who don't know me, I'm Loretha Grant, Trent's mother. I have known Brooke for four years, since my son came over, marveling about the woman he met at Outback Steakhouse." She turned to smile my way. "I don't think you know this, but my son was actually on a date with some scallywag."

"Mama!" Trent admonished.

Mrs. Grant waved him off. "I didn't like that girl, but Trent was always hardheaded."

"Is there a point to this story, Mama?" Trent's brother, Clark, called out as the room erupted in laughter.

"Hush, boy, and let me finish," she said. She turned her attention back to me. "Anyway, he told me that night that he tore up the scallywag's number because he'd met his wife. Of course, I didn't believe him, but I know my son, when he wants something, he goes after it. And he wanted you, Brooke Hayes."

Trent pulled me closer to him. "And I got her," he mumbled.

"And I'm so glad you did." Mrs. Grant raised her glass in a toast. "Brooke, I can't wait for you to become my daughter-in-law," she said. "I know you lost your mother when you were just a little girl, but I hope that you will see me as a second mother. To the happy couple."

I struggled to keep my smile as everyone raised their glasses in celebration. I liked Mrs. Grant, I really did. But she would never understand the depth of the love I had for my mother. And no one, not even her, would ever be able to replace that.

Trent pulled me to him and called out to his mother.

"Don't worry about that, Ma. I got her. And I have enough love that she won't miss a thing."

That made his mother smile even wider, and though I felt a piercing knot in my stomach, I smiled, too, and snuggled closer to my soon-to-be husband, hoping that he was right.

CHAPTER 2

....

*T*he sounds of the Dells filled the dining room. Lyrics about a house being a heart for love made the atmosphere festive. Pictures of the Grant children in every stage of life covered the walls. The Grant boys at a football game. The girls in dance clothes. The whole family at Easter. The wall was a museum of Grant family love. That, coupled with the incessant chatter of laughter, bickering, and joking made me feel like I was in the middle of a holiday celebration. But this was just a regular Sunday dinner at the Grants'.

It was a life I knew nothing about.

Our family dinners had consisted of me, my dad, grandma, and, on occasion, April and Uncle Clyde, who wasn't really my uncle but my father's best friend for forty years. Since my mother's death, there hadn't been much cause for celebration in our lives. In fact, the chair my mother had sat in every night at dinner remained empty throughout the years, some sort of shrine, reminding us all that she was gone. My grandmother had tried many times to move the chair, or even sit in it, but my father had been adamant that it was to remain empty.

For years that had made most of our dinners somber. That's why when I was old enough to work, I made it a point to have my schedule go through dinnertime.

Yeah, the joy that filled the Grant family had bypassed the Hayes residence.

"Carl, you know your daddy likes the breast." Mrs. Grant popped the back hand of her youngest son just as he stuck his fork into the giant piece of fried chicken at the center of the table. At eighteen, Carl was the baby of the family, and every time I'd been around him, he milked it for all that it was worth. Today, however, it obviously wasn't paying off.

"Mom, why Daddy always gotta have the breast?" he whined.

We all sat at the long dining room table. In addition to fried chicken, there was baked fish for Kendra, fried fish for Clark, macaroni and cheese for Carl, dirty rice for Trent, collard greens for Mr. Grant, corn bread and corn-on-the-cob for Kimala, and a host of other artery-clogging foods for everyone else. And Mrs. Grant had cooked every single dish. The feast in front of us had the Grant dinner table looking like it was Thanksgiving *and* Christmas. Glancing at the plethora of food, it suddenly dawned on me: I couldn't remember a time that my mother had cooked. I'm sure at some point she had to have, but I definitely didn't recall anything like this. That thought made me sad. The older I got, the harder time I had remembering anything about my mother. Twenty-five years had a way of erasing memories.

"When your name goes on the mortgage around here, you can have all the breasts you want," Trent's father said as he took his fork, stabbed the large piece of chicken, then picked it up and put it on his plate.

I brushed aside the melancholy feeling that often did its best to overpower me. I loved coming to Trent's house. The first Sunday of every month his mother was adamant about us all getting together, and even though we'd all had a long night last night at my engagement party, Mrs. Grant reminded Trent and me that we needed to be at her house by 2 p.m. I didn't mind because time with Trent gave me a glimpse into what it was like to have a big family, which I definitely wanted one day.

My father had an older sister, my cousin April's mother, who had died many years ago, and he had a distant cousin who visited from time to time. But other than that, our extended family was very small. So I relished being around Trent, his five siblings, and his mother and father. They were the movie *Soul Food* personified.

"Sorry I missed the engagement last night," Mr. Grant said. "But when you're the boss—"

"You gotta pick up the slack when others slack off." All five of his children spoke in unison. I joined in their laughter because I'd only been around the family three years and I knew Mr. Grant's infamous quote by heart, too. He ran a construction company and even though he was the boss, he worked from sunup to sundown.

A loud crash made all of our attention turn to the children's table, which was positioned in the corner of the large dining room.

Trent's nephew had knocked over a pitcher of Kool-Aid trying to hit his older brother.

"Demarcus, what have I told your bad behind?" Trent's sister, Kimala, snapped.

"You tell them everything under the sun. You just do nothing about it," Trent's other sister, Kendra, interjected.

The two of them were twins but they disputed any theories that twins had a natural bond. I don't think there had been a time that I'd been around the two of them that they didn't fight like Tyson and Holyfield.

Kimala's head whipped around and she raised a finger in her sister's direction.

"Oh, I'm sorry. Maybe I should raise some Stepford children like you got over there." She pointed to Kendra's two eight-year-old girls, who were sitting at the children's table like they were in a Miss Manners class. Their napkins were folded across their laps, their posture was perfect, and they looked disgusted at the behavior of their cousins.

Kendra didn't flinch. "It's called manners. Try it. Your kids might like it."

Kimala rolled her eyes. "We don't believe in stifling our children. We allow them to be creative."

Kendra returned the eye roll and punctuated it with a disgusting sigh. "That's code for run around batshit crazy."

"Look, today is supposed to be special," Mrs. Grant snapped at her children. "Y'all ruining the whole mood. Demarcus, sit your little behind down and finish your dinner before I get my switch."

Their argument took me back to one of the memories that was still vivid because it was one of the few times my mother had disciplined me.

· · · · · ·

"You're going to eat this food that I've been in here slaving over all day," my mother scolded.

I sat with my arms folded across my chest, defiant. "I. Don't. Want. Mashed. Potatoes."

We were sitting at the dinner table. Just the three of us, which was rare.

"I don't care what you want," my mother replied.

"She doesn't eat mashed potatoes, Sarah." My father sighed.

"She's six. She eats what we tell her to eat."

My father took my plate and scooped my mashed potatoes onto his plate. "There, Princess. Now eat your pork chops."

My mother slammed her hand on the table. "Why must you undermine everything I do? That's what's wrong with her. You spoil her and give her whatever she wants," my mother snapped. "And she knows you will take her side so she manipulates you."

"She's six," my father repeated. "She doesn't even know what manipulate means."

A mist covered my mother's eyes as she glared at my father. "We finally get a moment to ourselves with your mother gone and I try to do something nice for this family and nothing is ever good enough."

"Now you're being dramatic," my father casually replied, sliding a forkful of spinach into his mouth. "If you'd cook more often, you'd know that your daughter doesn't like mashed potatoes. Or spinach." He winked at me and I smiled. My daddy knew me so much better than Mommy.

"Stop spoiling her!"

Now I was wishing that I'd just eaten the mashed potatoes. I hated to give them any more reason to fight.

My father calmly set his fork down and pinched my cheek. "First of all, she's my princess and if I want to spoil her, I will." He directed his attention in my mother's direction. "Secondly, you're misdirecting your anger. You're mad at me and taking it out on her."

I didn't know what misdirecting meant, but it made my mother look at him like she wanted to take that fork he'd just set down and poke him in the eye with it.

Her voice was firm as she said, "I made dinner. I turned down the gig and I'm playing the dutiful housewife."

My father went back to eating. "I think it's pretty sad that you feel like that's a role you have to play . . ."

· · · · · · ·

"Brooke!"

I snapped out of my thoughts as Trent gripped my arm and shook it.

"Oww," I said, jerking my arm away. "That hurt."

"Sorry," he replied. "Mama was talking to you and it's like you zoned out."

I shook away my memories and turned to her. "I'm sorry, Mrs. Grant. I didn't hear you."

Her anger with her grandson was now replaced with one of her infectious smiles.

"I was just saying, how does it feel to be engaged?"

"It feels wonderful." I shivered. *Why had that memory affected me so?*

"Let me see that ring," Kimala said, reaching for my hand. I extended my arm and she almost snatched my hand off trying to get a good look at my ring. She studied it for a few seconds, then said, "That doesn't make any sense. That had to cost a grip. I thought you didn't make that much money," she said to her brother.

Trent narrowed his eyes at her. I knew that Kimala was the bold one of the family, but that question even caught me off guard.

"First of all, you don't need to worry about how much I make," Trent said.

Kimala shook her head like she wasn't convinced. "I know your little tech job ain't paying money like that."

"Ignore her, little bro," his brother Clark said, reaching for another scoop of macaroni and cheese. "Congratulations, you two. When is the wedding?"

Trent reached up and took my hand from his sister. "I don't know but we're going to set a date soon. I want to do it quickly."

Mrs. Grant's eyes widened in surprise as her hand went to her mouth to cover her squeal. "Oh, my God. Oh, my God. Are you pregnant? She's pregnant," she exclaimed, without giving me time to answer.

More chatter broke out across the room, with Demarcus singing, "Uncle Trent is gonna be a daddy, him and Brookie did the nastyyyy."

I ignored Demarcus, and the fact that no one chastised the seven-year-old, and said, "Hello! Can everyone slow down for a second. I am not pregnant."

No one seemed to be listening to me, though. Trent thought it was funny as his family went ballistic with excitement. Mrs. Grant's eyes teared up as if this would have been her first grandchild and not her eighth.

"Oh, my goodness. Oh, my goodness," she exclaimed, clapping her hands together. "I would have rather you two got married first. But a baby is a blessing no matter what. That explains why you're looking a little plump. I told Charlie you were pregnant, didn't I, baby?"

I decided to ignore her dig—because I'd been around her long enough to know that she didn't really mean anything by it.

"You called it, babe," her husband replied.

"I. Am. Not. Pregnant," I said as loud as possible.

"Oh." His mother lost her smile and the chatter died down. "It's just Trent said you were going to get married quickly," she said, confused.

Trent took a sip of his sweet tea, then said, "Mama, it's just quickly because I love her and I want us to go ahead and get married." He hesitated, and looked at me. "Before I reenlist."

"You're going back?" Clark exclaimed. An Afrocentric militant, Clark was opposed to all things military and made no secret of his disdain for his brother's commitment to this country.

All of us looked at Trent in shock. But no one was more shocked than me. Trent hadn't said a word to me about reenlisting. When he'd gotten out of the Navy, he'd taken a civilian job doing technology work for a local computer company. It was a great job, with great benefits, so I had no clue why he would want to leave it and reenlist. Not to mention that I had no desire to go live on a military base.

"Man, Uncle Sam got you whipped," Clark said. "The black man needs to be fighting for rights right here in our own country, not fighting some foreigners who haven't done anything to us."

"Oh, Lord. Please don't get Little Malcolm X started," Kimala said.

Trent must've known I was getting upset because he squeezed my hand and said, "It's just something I'm considering. But for now, I want to focus on marrying my love."

"Well, y'all don't need to be doing a big ol' wedding," Mr. Grant said. "Kendra did that, spent a luxury RV on a wedding, and was divorced a year later."

"Thanks, Dad, for reminding me," Kendra quipped.

He shrugged, unfazed. "I'm just saying. Don't make a bit

of sense to spend all that money so a bunch of other folks can see you tie the knot."

"We'd have something small, if we don't elope." I managed a smile even though it was taking everything to keep my attitude in check. At this point, we needed to discuss if there would even be a wedding.

Trent leaned in, gently kissed behind my earlobe, and whispered, "Don't be mad. I'm not going to do anything without talking to you."

Trent knew this was not something I was even willing to discuss. The reason why it had taken me months to even go out with him was that I had no desire to be that woman who opened the door to uniformed officers telling her her man had died while serving his country.

I knew that death was inevitable, but I didn't believe in opening the door to usher death in. As a sergeant, at the first sign of battle, Trent would be gone. And I'd drive myself crazy with worry, waiting on that call that my future had been snatched away. Again.

No, thanks.

"Well, let's change the subject," his mother announced. "I don't want to ruin dinner with heavy stuff."

I wanted to pull Trent aside so we could discuss this in detail, but he said, "Me either, Mama. Brooke has made me the happiest man ever and that's all I want to think about."

He kissed me again and just like that, I relaxed and smiled.

For now.

Because this conversation definitely wasn't over.

CHAPTER 3

$\mathcal{I}$t was ironic that the place I'd met my future husband was the place I was now sitting, contemplating how I'd ever see this marriage through. It had been a week since Trent proposed. Between that and the I'm-thinking-about-reenlisting-but-I-hadn't-decided-yet, I hadn't exactly been a blushing bride-to-be. In fact, we'd had a big blowup this morning about the reenlisting. I saw paperwork that he'd been filling out for housing at the base in Norfolk and I'd gone ballistic. That's why April had all but dragged me out to dinner, so I could "get away from the drama."

"Hey, Mark," I said, leaning in to look at the Outback name tag of our waiter. "Can you bring me another margarita, with salt?" Since my mother had been killed by a drunk driver, I had detested alcohol for years. In fact, I didn't start drinking until my midtwenties, and even now, seldom indulged. I guess that's why April was sitting across from me with a perched eyebrow.

"You want to slow down?" April asked. "We haven't even had dinner and you're on your second drink."

"Nope," I replied, giving Mark a would-you-hurry-up look.

"For someone that just had an amazing proposal, you sure don't act like it." She ran her hand across her belly as she sipped on lemon water. "Oooh. These babies are having a Gymboree session."

I smiled at the sight of her. Her little boy had swollen her petite frame to twice her normal size. But nobody who knew her sweated it. April was a health nut, so there was no doubt that any weight she gained from the baby would be gone in less than a month.

I couldn't wait to be a mother, to carry a child in my womb. Nurture and love them. There was something special about motherhood and for April, she was wearing it well.

"I can't believe you still have three months left," I said, grateful to get the attention off me.

"Girl, the doctor is talking about putting me on bed rest for the rest of my term. I am not about to go lay up in the bed all day so Sam can drive me crazy."

April's husband, Sam, worked from home. On the outside, they had the perfect marriage, but like any seemingly perfect marriage, behind closed doors they had their issues. Sam wanted April to be a stay-at-home mom, and April wanted to have it all. Her career as a pharmaceutical sales rep and motherhood.

"Anyway, don't try to change the subject," April continued. "We were talking about you—and your lack of excitement at getting married."

I downed the rest of my mango margarita, then set the glass back on the table. "I am excited. Trent is everything I've ever dreamed of."

And he was. When we first met, I had no desire to strike up

a relationship with a military man. And I'd known that because he was wearing his uniform in Outback, which I thought was real cheesy. I'd accused him of trying to finagle a free meal. Even though I'd given him my number, and we talked almost daily, he was still in the Navy and I was, therefore, uninterested. But then he'd gotten out, come home, and won my heart.

April narrowed her eyes, studied me, then said, "So why then do you not look like a happy bride? I remember the day Sam asked me to marry him. You would've thought I won the Powerball, the Mega Millions, and the Big Apple scratch-off. But you're acting like you've been sentenced to an arranged marriage. What's up with that?"

I had been asking myself that same question. If I loved Trent, why was I hesitant to get married? I was thirty-two. What woman didn't want to be married by thirty-two? Was it my aversion to forever? And if so, why had I paid that therapist all that money if I was still scared of love?

······

"Come on, Brooke. You've got to let him go."

"No, no, no," I sobbed, rocking back and forth like a woman on the verge of losing it. I hadn't moved from my seat since they'd lowered my fiancé into the ground. The cemetery groundskeeper was standing off to the side. He and his workers had empathetic expressions. I'm sure they'd seen their share of people who couldn't let go. And my name would just be added to the list.

I was supposed to be having my bachelorette party today. Instead I was putting my fiancé in the ground.

"Baby, the car is waiting," my father said.

"Why? Why do I lose everybody I love?" I cried.

My father took my hand. "You still have me."

"And me," April added, taking my other hand. The two of them hadn't left my side since I had gotten the news of Jared's death. I had taken it especially hard because I felt like it was my fault. I'd begged Jared to come over. I was feeling emotional about my mother not being at my wedding. He had so much to do but he'd come because I called. And on his way to my place, some thugs decided they wanted his Mustang. His pride and joy. And if I knew Jared, he resisted.

One fatal bullet altered the course of my life.

"You have to let him go," April said, gently squeezing my arm.

I knew they were right. All of the guests were gone. Even Jared's mother had left. I took a deep breath and stood just as a light sprinkle started.

God was joining me in my mourning.

I summoned up my strength and inched closer to the hole where Jared's body would spend eternal life. I tossed my one red rose into the hole and watched as it landed on top of Jared's casket.

"I will never love again," I mumbled.

· · · · · ·

"I am happy about marrying Trent," I said, struggling to bury the memory of Jared. "It's just . . ." My words trailed off as my hand instinctively went to my necklace.

April reached over and patted my other hand. "You're missing Jared and Aunt Sarah?"

I nodded. "You would think after all these years, it would be easy. But it's like I have a hole inside of me. I worked hard to heal that hole."

"Death is a part of life," she reminded me.

I sighed, knowing she was right. But if I didn't have that soul-loving love, I'd be better equipped to handle death.

"It's not just the forever thing with Jared," I continued. "I mean, do I really want to love someone like my dad did—to the point that you can't function once they're gone? And then, a wedding day is something you're supposed to share with your mother. It breaks my heart all over again that I won't get to do that." I swallowed the lump in my throat and fought back the tears welling up inside me.

April's mother, my daddy's sister, had also died when she was just a little girl, but her stepmother had done an awesome job and had become my de facto mother. Unfortunately, she and April's father had retired to Florida, so we didn't get to see them both much.

"Well, you know Aunt Sarah is up there looking down on you, proud as Michelle Obama's mama on Barack's Inauguration Day. She'll be there with you on your wedding day." April leaned in and tapped my heart. "She'll be right there."

That made me smile. Even though she was younger than me by two years, April had been the voice of reason all my life. And just that quickly, she had me feeling better.

"Now, come on, let's find a dress," April said, her mood shifting into planning mode as she grabbed a stack of magazines out of her tote bag. She set them on the table, brushed her spiral honey-blond curls out of her face, and flipped open the pages of the first magazine.

"I don't need all of that," I said, pointing to the stack of bridal magazines. "I told you I'm thinking about eloping."

"Girl, please." She studied me, I guess trying to see if I was serious. When she realized that I was, she said, "I cannot believe you are seriously going to elope. Who elopes these days?"

"People that don't want the pomp and circumstance of a wedding," I replied.

"Everybody wants a big wedding," April said.

"No. Your wedding was big enough for everyone in our family."

"It was kinda big, huh?" She laughed.

I was April's maid of honor. And she'd had ten bridesmaids. Her wedding had been the thing fairy tales were made of. I didn't need all of that.

"It's just me and my little small circle of friends," I replied. "Plus, it would look bad with Trent's side of the church packed and my side only having you, Dad, Grandma, and a couple of other people."

"I told you, you need to get some friends."

"I have friends. I just like to keep my circle small. Women can't be trusted."

"It's that negative mentality that keeps women from thriving and supporting each other," April chastised.

"Okay, okay, not all women," I admitted. "Just some."

Mark interrupted us when he came to set my drink on the table. "Ready to order?" he asked.

We placed our orders for the steak salad, then tossed around more honeymoon ideas. Even though my mind hadn't been right at first, by the time our salads came, I was completely on board.

In one of the magazines, I had just found the perfect dress—an ankle-length number that was just right for an informal ceremony, when my cell phone rang. I picked it up, frowned, and put it back down.

"Who was that?" April asked.

"I don't know. Unknown number. Ain't nobody got time for that," I joked.

She laughed, then minutes later, her phone rang. She

glanced at the phone, then pointed it toward me. The caller ID read the same, "Unknown."

"I can answer unknown numbers because I don't owe anyone." She winked as she pressed TALK. "Hello . . . What? Grandma, calm down." April sat straight up in her seat. "Yeah, she's here with me . . . what's going on?"

My heart dropped as I watched terror spread across my cousin's face.

"Okay . . . yeah . . . Duke Memorial? Got it, we're on our way."

"Oh, my God. Is Grandma all right?" My heart felt like it was preparing for an Olympic track meet. My grandmother had been living with us since I was four. She'd moved in after my grandfather died and had been there ever since.

April grabbed her purse, pulled out three twenties, and tossed them next to our plates. "We have to go." She pushed away from the table.

"What's going on, April?" I demanded, standing along with her. "What's wrong with Grandma?"

April took a deep breath and calmed herself, but her eyes were filling with terrified tears. "Grandma is fine." She reached across the table and took my hand. "It's your dad. They rushed him to the hospital."

I didn't wait for her to finish. I grabbed my purse and raced out of the restaurant.

CHAPTER 4

....

I channeled my high school track days as I raced through the doors of Duke Memorial.

The nurse at the front desk greeted me with a smile as if I had just stopped in my favorite restaurant to place an order for food. "Good evening, may I help you?" she said.

"Yes, I'm looking for my father, Jacob Hayes, they just brought him in."

My panicked expression wiped her smile away as she turned and began pecking on her keyboard. She leaned in and peered at the screen. "Graham, Green, Hamilton, Hayes. There he is. Yes, he's in room 212. Right down—"

I didn't give her time to direct me and just took off down the hall. I had just rounded the corner when I saw my grandmother standing in the waiting room, tears in her eyes. Her Bible was clutched to her chest and she was mumbling what I knew was a fervent prayer. Everything morphed into slow motion. I opened my mouth to speak but no words came out.

"Is . . . Is . . ."

"Is Uncle Jacob okay?" April asked, stepping in to finish my sentence. I had left her in the parking lot, but I was thankful that she'd caught up with me. She took my hand to steady me. She must have known my knees were on the verge of giving out.

"He is." My grandmother's voice vibrated with fear. "They have him on a ventilator. It's not looking good."

"What happened?" April and I spoke at the same time.

Slow tears trickled down her face. My grandmother was the epitome of a strong matriarch. I'd only seen her cry once in my lifetime—at my grandfather's funeral. So this sight put my stomach in knots.

"He had a stroke," she said.

"A stroke?" I gasped. I had been motherless all of my life. Was I about to be fatherless, too?

April's hand went to her stomach as if the news had punched her in the gut. "It's all that fatback Uncle Jacob eats," she muttered.

"I've been eating the fat off the back for eighty-six years and I'm fine," my grandmother snapped.

"Okay, Granny, calm down," April said.

My grandmother took a deep breath and began pacing the waiting room. "I'm sorry, baby. It's just my nerves are so bad. I came downstairs and found Jacob laid out on the floor, barely breathing. My heart almost gave out right there, too. I lost Ray from a stroke. I can't lose my only son."

"Granddaddy died from hypertension?" April asked. "And you didn't change your eating hab—"

I shot April a "Not the time" look and she quickly shut up.

"Sorry," April mumbled. "Let's just pray for Uncle Jacob. He's gonna be fine."

"He is," I said, nodding as if that would make it so. "I need to see him."

"He's back there," Grandma said. "His doctor, Dr. Toobin, asked us to wait here until someone comes and gets us. I think they've got him stabilized but I just can't see him like that."

Honestly, neither could I. I couldn't bear the thought of losing my father . . . like I'd lost my mother. All of us must have been thinking the same thing, because a deathly silence filled the room, allowing morbid memories to take over.

· · · · · ·

I clutched the flowers, squeezing the stems to the point that I thought they'd break in half. I didn't know how I even had the strength to stay steady on my feet. The only comforting grace was my father's strong hand gripped tightly on my shoulders. He had talked to me about how I had to be strong. But how could I be strong when my mommy was dead?

I willed the tears away. Unfortunately, my body wouldn't sync with my mind and the tears I'd been trying so hard not to let loose burst free. My father squeezed my shoulder tighter. My grandmother moved in and took my hand.

"And so today, we gather to say goodbye to Sarah Hayes."

I looked at the 11x17 picture of my mother, which sat on the table at the front of the room. It was my favorite photo. And now, it would be all that I would have.

"You'll have your memories, too, baby." Daddy had told me that just this morning. But I didn't want memories. I wanted my mommy. I wanted to go back to the time when Mommy would take me to play in the park. We didn't do stuff like that a lot (I didn't really know why), but I loved whenever we did.

"Ashes to ashes . . . dust to dust . . ."

I looked around our living room. I still didn't understand why we were having Mama's funeral here—or why Uncle Clyde was performing the ceremony. He wasn't a preacher, at least I didn't think he was. I also didn't know why none of Mommy's friends were here. Not that she had many friends . . . she didn't work and she didn't get out much, but even her friend Denise was nowhere to be found.

"She's too broken up, she can't handle it," Daddy had said when I asked him about it right before the service started.

There must not have been many people that could handle it because nobody was here to say goodbye to my mommy but me, Daddy, Grandma, and Uncle Clyde. Daddy said that was the way Mommy had wanted it. He called it a private memorial service, with no fuss. Just something small and intimate to say goodbye.

My pudgy little hands trembled as I thought about the fact that I never got to say goodbye. Mommy had gone to the store and simply never come back. A drunk driver had plowed into her car, killing her instantly.

Mommy's death had made Daddy incredibly sad. He had tried to be strong and not tell me what happened, but I heard him in his room crying and breaking everything in sight, he was so upset. He finally had to tell me the truth.

Today, however, he hadn't shed a tear, and I knew it was all because of me. Daddy needed to be strong to help me be strong. That's what he had told me this morning. I guess Granny was trying to be strong, too. She hadn't shed a tear, either.

"Until you meet again," Uncle Clyde said. "May you rest in eternal peace."

My heart broke and I fell to the floor in a heap of tears. I was scared of dying, but I would be happy when death finally came so that I could see my mommy again.

. . . . . .

No one knew how much that day had shaped me. The reason the memory was so vivid was that I had relived it ten thousand times over the past twenty-five years.

I glanced up at the clock on the waiting-room wall. They really needed to get rid of it because all it did was remind people of how long they had been waiting. In our case, three hours.

That's why when I saw the nurse enter, I all but leapt out of my seat.

"The doctor said one of you can go back."

Of course, April and my grandmother turned to me. I didn't reply as I took off.

As I rushed down the hall, the hospital smell assaulted my nose, causing my nerves to tense up even more. I slowed my pace when I reached room 212.

"God, please let him be okay," I mumbled before pushing open the door to his room.

The sight of my father lying in that bed, his eyes closed, tubes coming out of his nose, the slow drone of the monitor beeping as if it were a countdown to his demise, made me sick to my stomach. A nurse was standing over his bedside checking an electronic chart. She nodded a silent greeting, then tiptoed out of the room.

I took slow steps toward my father, trying my best not to break down into a ball of tears. My heart dipped with each step I took.

"Hey, Daddy," I whispered. The slow drone was the only reply. I summoned up every iota of strength as I took his hand. "I heard you had a rough time today, but everything is going to be fine. I need you to get better. I'm about to get married, remember? I know we talked about eloping, but I'm still walking down the aisle and you have to give me away. I can't do it if you're not there."

My father really liked Trent, had liked him since the first time he met him. He told me he had prayed for a man like Trent for me. I could only hope seeing me marry Trent would be enough to get him to pull through. I would even agree to a big wedding if he would just promise to be there.

My father was a fighter. I'd seen that over the years—when a teacher wronged me, when a classmate bullied me, when someone tried to take advantage of him. The only place I'd ever seen an iota of weakness was behind my mother. Right now I needed Daddy to summon up all of his strength, fight through this, and come back to me.

"Daddy, can you hear me?" I whispered.

The drone continued, piercing the silence of the room.

"Don't leave me." I echoed my father's words that he used to mutter while he cradled my mother's picture for years after her death.

A slow sob built inside me, then snowballed, funneled by my anguish, until it verbalized into a painful wail with the thought of losing my father.

"Daddy, please be okay," I cried as I buried my head into his chest.

I felt something on my head and I jumped. My tears of anguish turned to tears of joy when I realized my father was stroking my hair.

"Oh, my God, Daddy. You're okay." I caressed his head. I had never been so grateful to see him open his eyes.

The oxygen mask covered his nose and mouth but he managed a slight nod.

"I was so worried." I leaned up and kissed his forehead. He struggled to remove his mask. I gently grabbed his hand to stop him. "No, Daddy, leave that alone. Let me get a nurse."

He shook his head and gripped my arm to keep me from leaving.

"I . . . I need to . . ." His words were muffled by his mask and I could barely make them out.

"No, you need to rest." I broke free and ran to the door. "Nurse! My dad's awake."

The medical team rushed in and immediately began examining my father. His arms flailed as he kept trying to remove the mask, but the nurse grasped his hands, trying to keep him calm.

After a few minutes, the doctor hung his stethoscope around his neck, then stood erect. "Mr. Hayes, you gave us quite a scare. But we've managed to get your blood pressure down and get all your vitals stabilized. You're not out of the woods yet. It's touch-and-go so we need you to rest. We'll keep this IV flowing but you cannot exert any energy."

My dad didn't seem to be listening to the doctor. He kept trying to reach for me. "Br . . ."

"Daddy, please."

My father struggled to sit up, his arms outstretched toward me. "I-I'm s-sorry . . ."

"Mr. Hayes, you have to take it easy," the doctor admonished.

I eased closer to him. "Would you stop? You have nothing to be sorry for. You have no control over your heart."

"Not. That." He gasped, wheezed, and still tried to sit up. But immediately fell back down. "I-I'm just s-sorry." Just that minuscule effort seemed to have drained him of all his energy.

Dr. Toobin put a hand on my shoulder. "I'm sorry, I'm going to have to ask you to leave. We need to keep him stabilized."

The frantic expression on my father's face was frightening. But the doctor was right, my presence was getting him worked up.

"I'll be right outside, Daddy," I said.

He was too weak to do anything other than lie there. I eased out of the room as two nurses worked to calm my father.

My father had always been the epitome of cool. But one thing he seldom did was apologize. I stood in the hallway trying to think of the last time he'd ever said, "I'm sorry." I couldn't recall. Then it dawned on me; the only other time was during a fight days before my mother disappeared.

. . . . . .

"I'm sorry, okay? Is that good enough for you?"

My mother hadn't replied and my grandmother had come in the room so I never got to hear what he was apologizing for.

. . . . . .

Other than that, the stubborn part of him rarely let him apologize. That's why his words continued swirling in my head. I approached my grandmother. My nerves were frazzled.

"How is he?" she asked.

"Daddy woke up," I replied.

"What?" April exclaimed, wobbling in an effort to stand up.

"Praise the Lord!" my grandmother cried.

"He kept getting worked up and he kept trying to apologize."

My grandmother's eyes grew wide. "For what?"

I shrugged. "He just kept saying 'I'm sorry.' You know Daddy doesn't do that so what in the world could he be talking about?"

The way my grandmother's shoulders slumped made my heart beat faster.

"Did he know he was dying?" I demanded to know. "Is that what he's talking about? He's sorry for not telling me that he was sick?"

She shook her head harder. "I don't know, baby. We can't worry about that now. All we can do now is pray, pray that your daddy gets better. I'm going to the chapel to pray." She darted out of the lobby before I could ask any more questions.

CHAPTER 5

*T*his had been the longest twenty-four hours of my life.
Both April and my grandmother had gone home to
get some rest. Now they were back, along with Trent, trying
to get me to go home for a little while.

What they didn't understand was if I left and my daddy
died, I'd never be able to go home again.

I mean, I hadn't lived at home for twelve years, but my
father's house would always be home. And if I had no father,
I'd have no home.

Daddy had taken a turn for the worse right after trying
to talk to me and all night, every time a nurse or doctor
headed in my direction, my heart plummeted in morbid anticipation.

Trent walked over and hugged me for the twentieth time.
"Babe, are you sure you don't want me to take you home? You
can shower and get something to eat, because these chips from
the snack machine aren't going to cut it," he said.

I pushed him away, a little harder than I meant to. "I'm.
Not. Leaving. So please stop asking," I snapped.

He released a defeated sigh.

Trent didn't get it. No one did. My dad was all I had. After my mother died, it was just me and him against the universe. He'd never remarried. Over the years I had seen several women at church try to come on to him, but he wasn't having it. Once, when I was sixteen, I overheard he and Uncle Clyde talking.

"Man, I can't believe you're gonna let that fine Bonnie Carothers get away," Uncle Clyde had said.

"She is fine, isn't she?" my daddy replied. Ms. Bonnie showed up at our house on a regular basis—in the beginning, to borrow a cup of sugar, or some milk, or some cream. It never made sense to me because she lived the next neighborhood over and had to pass the corner store to get to our house. After a while, she stopped pretending she needed to borrow something and would just show up, trying to invite herself to dinner. My father always made excuses and eventually, she just stopped trying.

"Every man this side of the Triangle wants that woman and she wants you," Uncle Clyde said.

"Yeah, but Brooke—"

"Brooke is dang near grown." Uncle Clyde cut him off. "In a few months, she'll be gone off to school and you'll be all alone."

"I'm alone, not lonely."

A silence hung between them before Uncle Clyde said, "It's Sarah?" He didn't give my dad time to answer before he said, "Man, you've got to let her go."

"I can't. She's the love of my life." I could hear the pain in his voice. I think that's the first time I decided I didn't want to know love like that. I didn't want to love someone so hard that no one could ever take their place in my heart once they were gone.

Uncle Clyde obviously was not moved by my father's proc-
lamation because he said, "The love of your life is gone. And
no matter how much you keep hoping, she ain't coming back.
It's time to move on."

"Would you hush before Brooke overhears you?"

That conversation had made me so sad. My father had never
gotten over my mother's death. And we never talked about it.
Truthfully, it made us both so sad. But sometimes, even all
these years later, I wish we could talk about her, reminisce,
anything. But it's like my father wanted her wiped out of our
minds and hearts. I guess it was just too painful for him.

"How's he doing?" I jumped up as my grandmother walked
back into the waiting room. When she'd returned from home
a few hours ago, she finally had the courage to go and sit with
him for a while. The puffiness and redness of her eyes told me
that the visit hadn't gone well.

"He's dying." My grandmother sobbed. "My baby is dying."

Trent stood and took my grandmother into his arms. I
know that I should have gone to hug her, too, but I was frozen
in place. I couldn't move. I don't know what I was expecting,
maybe for her to say some miracle had taken place. That the
God that she worshipped faithfully, and that I had all but given
up on when He took my Jared, would prove Himself worthy
and restore my father.

My grandmother composed herself as she released herself
from Trent's embrace. "His brain is swelling. They are going
to rush him into surgery. The doctor asked that I come get the
family so . . ." She fanned herself with both hands as she swallowed the lump in her throat. "So . . . we can say goodbye,
just in case."

"No!"

I hadn't even realized the words had come out of my mouth. My grandmother looked too exhausted to argue. "Either you can say goodbye now. Or you can wait and do it at his funeral."

His funeral.

The words caused my legs to crumble, and Trent raced to keep me from tumbling to the floor.

"It's okay, babe," he said, helping steady me. "I'm right here. I'll help you through this."

I don't know how, but Trent guided my wobbly legs down the long hallway and into my father's room. The drone continued humming, louder this time, like it was mocking my dad. My father looked even more frail than he had when I was in here six hours ago.

"I'll wait right here," Trent said just outside my father's hospital room door.

"Hey, Daddy." I managed a smile as I approached his bed. I was just grateful to see his eyes half-open. They had removed the mask and replaced it with tubing.

My father tried to lift a hand, but the exertion of energy proved too much and he dropped it back onto the bed.

I eased over and took his hand into mine. "I love you. Forever."

"A . . . n . . . d e . . . ver." Although his voice was just above a whisper, him uttering our favorite way of saying I love you made me want to climb into his bed and die right along with him.

"You're gonna be okay," I said, rubbing his salt-and-pepper hair. I know I didn't sound convincing, but maybe if I said it enough, it would come true.

He shook his head, causing my tears to flow even faster. "I-I have to t-tell you someth—"

I stopped him. "No, you just have to be quiet and get better. The doctors are working hard and they're going to save your life, you hear me? I prayed to God."

Though he looked absolutely worn out, my father managed a slight smile. If he were in his right mind, he probably would've jumped for joy. Despite the fact that he had me in church every Sunday, the minute I left for college, I started drifting away. Then, when Jared died, I'd left the church altogether. I had never reconciled a God who would allow so much pain and suffering. It's not that I didn't believe in God. I just had a lot of questions no one had been able to answer, so I'd drifted away from organized religion and become more of a spiritual person—which, of course, drove my grandmother mad.

"You may have left God, but He didn't leave you," my father had told me just last Sunday. I hoped he was right because I'd prayed all night. And hopefully, God was listening and would save my daddy.

I tried to put strength behind my words. "You always say everything happens for a reason. You're in this hospital because God wanted to show me His healing power."

I heard my grandmother grunt in the background. I hadn't even heard her come in. "You're going to come through this surgery just fine," I continued.

"N-no, I won't . . . but k-know I'm so . . . rry . . ." His whispered apologies brought even more tears to my eyes.

Now my interest was really piqued.

"I only w-wanted wh-what's best."

The nurse walked in before I could reply.

"I am sorry to cut you all off but we have got to get Mr. Hayes into surgery. The doctor is prepped and ready to go."

Grandma leaned down and kissed my father on the head. "I'll tell her," I heard my grandmother whisper. "I promise."

"Tell me what?" I couldn't help but ask.

But before my grandmother could respond, my father squeezed her hand, then his arm dropped to his side as his eyes rolled into the back of his head. I was momentarily discombobulated as I tried to figure out what was happening. But then that horrible flatline sound that I had heard in numerous movies permeated the air. I screamed. My grandmother stood frozen. Then the nurse frantically rushed us out as I heard someone else yell, "Code Blue!"

Several nurses and the doctor came racing down the hall. They shuttled us out of the room as it turned into a whirlwind of chaos.

I watched through the hospital room window, trembling in silent fear as they connected contraptions to him, pumped his chest, shouted orders. They moved as fast as my heart. And then, all of the frantic movement stopped. Dr. Toobin's shoulders drooped and I saw him look at the clock. I couldn't tell what he was saying, but when I saw a nurse pull the cover over my father's now-lifeless body, I reached down deep inside my soul and released a blood-curdling scream that would change my world forever.

CHAPTER 6

They say that there is life after death. I don't know how. Because right about now, I didn't know how in the world I was supposed to keep living now that my daddy was dead.

I know it was crazy. I knew that we all had to die at some point, but to me, my father was invincible. Maybe if I had had time to prepare, to come to grips with this, I could've handled it better. But right about now I was handling this in the worst way possible. Another unexpected death of someone I loved.

"You ready, babe?" Trent looked gorgeous in his white Navy uniform. He had been so patient with me this past week. I had barely been able to function. Thankfully, April and my grandmother had stepped in and taken care of all of the funeral arrangements.

"No, I'm not ready," I replied, sitting on the edge of my childhood bed. I brushed down my black silk dress, which I knew I would give to Goodwill after today because I would never be able to wear it again. "Not ready," I repeated. "But we can go." Even as I said the words, I couldn't move.

Trent reached down, grabbed my arm, and pulled me up. "Come on, babe. You have to get it together. We can't be late."

I snatched my arm away. "Really?" I snapped. Today was not the day for his need for control. I would move at my own pace.

His shoulders relaxed as he pulled me to him, a lot more gentle this time. "I'm sorry, it's just the longer you sit here, the harder this is going to be. And we really need to get going. But I got you. I'll be here for you every step of the way."

Trent hugged me, I know, hoping to transfer some of his strength. It didn't work, though my irritation at his aggression did dissipate.

With bated steps, I made my way out into the living room, where April and her husband, my grandmother, Uncle Clyde, and one of my dad's cousins were all standing around. The air of grief suffocated the room.

"The cars are ready," the funeral-home director said. I took in his appearance. It was obvious he was in the right line of work. With his somber expression, hollow-looking eyes, and ashy face, he looked like something straight out of a horror movie.

Everyone waited for me to lead the way, which I did.

MY DADDY'S SERVICE WAS a blur. I remember the choir singing "Soon and Very Soon" and some other song that caused wails throughout the church. Several people spoke—many sharing funny moments about my father. But nothing anyone said could replace the sorrow that had consumed me.

When I wasn't shedding silent tears, I sat stoic, praying that I would wake up from this nightmare.

As the minister closed out the service, I heard my grand-mother let out a wail and that was my trigger, too. I felt the air seep from my body and everything around me went black.

I HAD NO IDEA how I got home, but when I came to, I was nestled in my childhood bed and the sun was peeking in through the blinds.

I sat up, stretched, and tried to get my bearings. I was still in my dress. The clock on the nightstand said it was 6 a.m. I pulled the covers back, got up, and headed into the bathroom to wash my face.

After I'd refreshed and changed into a maxi-dress that I'd left in my bedroom closet, I made my way into the kitchen.

I wasn't surprised to see my grandmother at the kitchen table, drinking coffee and reading the newspaper. It was an early morning ritual that she'd been doing for as long as I could remember.

"Good morning," she said when she saw me enter.

"Good morning." I slid in the seat across from her. "I can't believe I've been asleep for so long."

My grandmother got up and walked over to the coffeepot to pour me a cup. I wanted to tell her I'd much rather gour-met coffee from the Keurig I'd bought her for Christmas, but since she refused to use "that ridiculous contraption," I didn't bother saying anything.

"Trent gave you a sleeping pill. After you fainted, you came to but you were inconsolable and out of it. He brought you here and stayed till about midnight." She set the coffee cup down in front of me.

"I missed the burial." I picked the cup up and took a sip, hoping the heat could stave off my tears.

"That's probably best. You were in pretty bad shape."

We sat in silence for a moment, before I said, "Grandma, before Daddy died, he kept saying he was sorry. You said you would tell me something. What was he talking about?"

My grandmother hesitated, like she was contemplating whether she was going to say anything. She moved over to the stove and stood with her back to me.

"Grandma, please. I need to know. What did he mean?" I had been meaning to ask her about this all week, but I'd been so out of it, I forgot about it until now.

Her shoulders sank, as if whatever it was I needed to know weighed a ton. "Some secrets are best left buried," she said, her voice soft as she turned around.

"Secrets? Daddy and I didn't have any secrets from each other."

She refused to look at me as her eyes darted all around the kitchen, so I moved to stand directly in front of her.

"Tell me the truth," I said. "Was he sick and hiding it?"

Again, her shoulders rose, then fell. Finally, she shook her head. "No, the stroke caught all of us by surprise." She began pacing back and forth. It felt like she was just trying to escape my gaze. "Maybe we should give it some time."

I was out of patience and time. I put a hand on her arm to stop her pacing. "Grandma, no disrespect, but you need to tell me what's going on."

"I don't *need* to do anything but stay black and die," she said, jerking her arm away. She paced some more, then released a long sigh. "But it's about high time you knew. In fact, I thought you should've known a long time ago, but your daddy, he just . . ."

"Grandma, please?"

Our eyes met, she stared at me for a moment, then she turned and walked over to the armoire in the dining room. She pulled open a drawer, reached in, fumbled around, then pulled out a manila envelope. The intensity on her face as she walked back toward me sent my heart into a sprint.

With careful purpose, she opened the envelope and slid a photo in my direction. The woman in the picture was wearing the prettiest fuchsia dress and immediately I recognized the eyes. They were the eyes of the picture that sat on my nightstand. The same eyes that I said I love you to every night before I closed my eyes.

"Is this Mama?" I asked, my voice soft.

She nodded.

"She looks so much older." I was still trying to process why my dad had an old picture of my mom hidden away in an envelope in the drawer. I kept my picture, but after Daddy got rid of the photo he had held on to for years, he never had any more pictures of Mama around the house. He'd said it was too hard to see her face on a regular basis.

Now my grandmother was looking me straight in the eyes. "That's because she *is* older."

"What?"

My grandmother inhaled, exhaled, and then rushed her words out. "Baby, that's your mama."

It was then that I noticed the date stamp in the corner of the picture. "This says March 19, 2015."

She nodded.

Now I was utterly confused. My mother had been dead twenty-five years. "I don't understand. What's going on?"

"That picture is from two years ago."

I frowned, her words trying to register in my head. "I don't understand. Mama has been dead for years."

My grandmother fell back into her chair as if the delivery of this news was exhausting. "No, she hasn't."

"What?" I said. "Grandma, you're not making any sense."

Another long sigh, then she said, "Your mother isn't dead."

"I don't understand," I repeated, staring at the picture again. "This is crazy. My mother *is* dead."

Again, she just shook her head.

I continued: "I mean, we had a funeral. Remember?"

"No, we had a *memorial* service to remember her," my grandmother corrected.

Now it was my turn to pace. I shook the photo at my grandmother as I walked back and forth across the linoleum floor. "I'm not crazy. What kind of game is this? My mother has been dead for years."

"That's what we led you to believe. That's what we *wanted* you to believe."

I stopped pacing and stared at my grandmother in disbelief. "She's alive?" I don't know which was greater, the pain of my mother dying or the pain of knowing she was alive.

"What happened to her?" I demanded to know. "Where is she? Was she kidnapped? Did she have amnesia?" A lifetime of Lifetime movies ran through my head, searching for some viable explanation.

"Sit down," my grandmother said.

"No, I don't want to sit down. I want to know what's going on." Normally, I would've never been defiant to my grandmother, but these were extenuating circumstances.

My grandmother must've given me a pass on my defiance because she simply said, "Your mother ran away."

My brow furrowed as I said, "Children run away. Mothers don't run away."

"Your mother did."

My grandmother sipped some more of her coffee, then continued talking. "For the longest, I could tell your mother wasn't happy, but your father loved her so much. I think he thought he could force her to be happy. And for a minute, after you were born, you brought her some happiness. And then, it's like the light went out in her eyes. She just didn't want to be here. Obviously, this wasn't the life that she wanted."

I fell back against the kitchen counter, trying to process everything my grandmother was saying. "Okay, so then she gets a divorce." I had a lot of friends whose parents were divorced. *Most* of my friends' parents were divorced.

"Your mother knew that if she filed for divorce, she wouldn't be able to take care of you," my grandmother replied.

"That's crazy. They could've shared joint custody. Daddy would've paid child support." I paused. "Did Daddy do something to her?"

"Now, you wait a minute," Grandma said, getting angry. "It wasn't your daddy's fault. Sarah didn't *want* joint custody. She didn't want *any* custody. She wanted out. So she left to visit a friend one day and just never came back."

"Huh?" I had heard stories of back in the day, fathers who went to the store for bread and never returned. But this, a mother abandoning a child? That was insane. Mothers don't abandon their children.

I finally sat back down at the table. "So, my mother decided she didn't want to be a mother and you guys thought the answer was to pretend she was dead?"

"I didn't say it was right. Your daddy didn't want you to have to deal with the thought of your mother abandoning you."

"No." I shook my head. "I refuse to believe this."

She took another sip of her coffee. "Well, you can believe it, or not. But you know I don't lie. No need to."

I glared at my grandmother. "Except when it comes to making me believe my mother is dead."

The stunned expression on my grandmother's face made me immediately regret my words. But before I could apologize, she pushed back from the table and stood up.

"I'm going to chalk your disrespect up to grief and shock. But I'll leave you be now before I have to attend another funeral."

Anger pierced her steps as she made her way out of the kitchen. I would definitely apologize later. Right now, my mind was consumed with emotions—grief over losing my father, and excitement over the idea of finding my mother. The problem was I had no idea where to begin looking for her.

CHAPTER 7

For the past week, it had been a monumental effort just to do the most basic of tasks. I'd gone home and tried to get myself together, but when I saw the pile of clothes in my bedroom, I remembered that I hadn't washed since my father died. I went to toss a load of colored clothes in the washing machine, then poured bleach into the water.

I immediately realized what I was doing and was able to snatch some of my clothes out of the washer, but not before ruining my favorite jeans. I knew there was no way I'd be able to do anything with this revelation about my mother hanging over me.

Both April and Trent had called to check on me, but I needed to be alone. I hadn't told either of them my grandmother's news because I was still processing everything. But I knew that after yet another sleepless night, I had to find answers.

In fact, I told myself that I was going to get answers if it was the last thing I did. It seemed that my grandmother had given all that she had to give. I don't know if she was mad about my comment—even though I'd apologized. But she was adamant that she didn't know any more than what she'd told me. She didn't even know where the photo she had shown me had been taken. I'd studied it for hours, searching for some type of clue. Of course, there was nothing there. It was just a generic snapshot of her sitting on a park bench. But someone had to have taken the picture. Maybe my father had hired a private eye and he'd found my mother, and had taken the picture.

If my grandmother didn't have answers, I needed to head to the one other person who surely would—my father's best friend of forty years, Clyde Samuels.

That's why I had just pulled into his dilapidated driveway, which was stocked with old lawn mowers, ice makers, and everything in between. He was a Mr. Fix-It Man who never quite got around to fixing things, but that didn't stop him from collecting things to work on later.

"Well, hey, baby girl," he said as I made my way up the walkway. He was sitting on his front porch working on an air conditioner.

"Hi, Uncle Clyde." I kissed him on his cheek, his stubble scratching my lips.

Uncle Clyde was single and loving it. I couldn't for the life of me understand how an eighty-year-old man could pull in the women like he did. But ever since his wife died twenty-three years ago, that's exactly what he had been doing.

"Isn't this a pleasant surprise?" he said. He used his wrench to pat the chair next to him. "Sit. So what brings you by?"

I moved the toaster out of the way and took a seat. "I know I was out of it at the funeral, but I just wanted to check in and see how you were doing."

"The fact that I'm still here with all my faculties in order means I'm doing quite well." He narrowed his eyes at me. "But I am wondering why you're lying to me. Because you'll call me without hesitation, but it's been a while since you graced my humble abode."

I managed a smile as I looked around his yard. "You know all this clutter gives me hives?"

"Which is exactly why I live alone. Don't need no woman, no offense, in here telling me how to clean my house."

"I know, Uncle Clyde."

He grinned to let me know all was well. "You want something to drink? I can make you a gin and Coke."

"Uncle Clyde, it's ten in the morning."

"But it's almost midnight in China."

"Well, we're not in China."

"Suit yourself." He reached down on the side of his chair, grabbed a bottle, then poured some gin into a glass cup that had melting ice in it. He swirled the glass around, then took a sip.

"What happened to the Coke?"

"Well, the Coke is only for guests. I like my drink straight." He downed the whole drink and I grimaced for him.

"Now seriously, what's going on? You missing your daddy? You need to talk?"

"Well, you know I'm missing him. It's just so hard."

"I know." He got nostalgic and choked back his words. "I didn't know how much I loved that old geezer until he wasn't there for me to fight with."

That brought a smile to my face. And fight they did. Constantly. You would've sworn they were blood brothers the way they argued. But they wouldn't dare let anyone else talk bad about the other.

He slapped his knee, trying to snap himself out of his sorrow. "So, what's going on?"

I released a heavy sigh. "Uncle Clyde. I need some answers."

He leaned back. "You got questions. I got answers."

"About my mama?"

He sat upright, a surprised look across his face. "Umm, I don't know nothing about that."

"Come on, Uncle Clyde. Daddy apologized before he died. At the hospital, he just kept saying he was sorry. I didn't know why and Grandma told me that my mother is still alive and he was apologizing for lying and telling me otherwise."

I had uttered those words a thousand times since I found out and they were no less painful.

His sigh seemed to be a mixture of relief and sadness. "Yeah, I've been telling Jacob for years this day was gonna come."

"I don't understand. Why would Daddy keep something like that from me?" That's the question I'd been asking all night, right next to where was my mother.

Uncle Clyde took my hand.

"You know you were the most important thing in the world to your father. You were his life. I stayed single because I didn't like women for too long. But he stayed single because he didn't want to share his world with anybody other than you. He didn't want to share his heart with anybody but your mama."

"So, what happened? What made her leave?"

He dropped my hand and leaned back like he was thinking. "Well, don't rightly know. Honestly, I don't think she ever wanted to marry your father in the first place. She just never loved him the way a wife is supposed to love a husband. Your mother had a rough upbringing and I think she married him out of gratitude. She had been arrested and your daddy came along and was like a knight in shining armor."

"Arrested? My mother had a criminal record?" This was all too much. Not only was my mother alive somewhere, but she was a criminal?

He nodded. "Yeah. He was her ticket out of poverty and that jacked-up life. Jacob couldn't see it, though." Uncle Clyde shook his head. "My heart used to hurt so bad for my friend. He tried so hard and your mother was so unhappy. No, she was miserable. Yep, miserable is more like it."

"I just don't remember her being miserable," I said.

"Oh, she hid it well. At least around you. But behind closed doors, she let him have it. Behind closed doors she let him know how unhappy she was. And it used to tear his heart up. I don't think I have ever seen a woman rip a man to his core. I'm not even going to lie. I came to hate your mama. I saw what she was doing to my friend and it burned me up. I told him to leave her many times, but love"—he tsked in disgust—"love can turn you into a bona fide fool. And your daddy was a fool for love."

"So what happened? Grandma said she went to visit a friend and just never came back. There has to be more to it than that."

"Wish there was," he said, "then maybe your daddy wouldn't have been so tortured. That's what was killing him, the fact that he couldn't understand. He couldn't fathom what would drive her to leave y'all, especially you. Wanting out from him is one thing; leaving you is something he could never process."

There were no words to describe the pain in my heart. "Did he just let her go?" I asked.

I could see Uncle Clyde reaching back into his memory. "First, he thought something bad had happened," he said. "Your daddy called the police, the sheriff's office, the dog catcher, everybody. He moved heaven and earth trying to find her. For about three days he wouldn't eat, drink, or sleep. He worried the police. He searched databases. He drove up and down every street in Raleigh, camped out at hospitals. And then, she called. Just said she couldn't do it. Said she was fine, but she wanted out. He begged and pleaded and she told him to just forget she existed."

"And so, she just forgot I existed?" I all but whispered.

He shrugged. "Some people just don't have a mother's gene. I don't think that Sarah did."

"Then why did she have me? Why didn't she just have an abortion?"

"Oh, not having you was never an option. Your daddy had been told he had some . . . some man problems and couldn't have kids. Then Sarah got pregnant with you and he called you his miracle baby. Sarah would've had to kill him before he would've let her kill you. Plus, I don't think that was in her. I think there was a part of her that hoped you could help save their marriage, bring them some happiness, and for a while, you did. But there was never that connection. He did more caring and nurturing of you than she did."

"I don't remember any of that." With the exception of a few vivid recollections, the memories of my mother had faded over the years, but I definitely didn't recall feeling like my mother didn't care for me.

"Yeah, your mama was good at faking." The anger in Uncle Clyde's voice was palpable. "That's why me and your grandmother went along with the charade that she was dead, because truthfully, we thought both of y'all were better off without Sarah."

Something was missing. This wasn't adding up. "Was she on drugs or something?" There had to be something that would drive my mother to just leave, and the only thing I could think of was drugs.

He laughed. "Yeah, your daddy swore she had some kind of secret cocaine habit that was clouding her judgment. So he hired a private detective, tracked her down. Found out she was living in New York. He went to see her. Found her as a backup dancer for some singer—you know dancing was her thing. And she all but told him to leave her alone. So he did. He didn't want to drag her back. He feared that she'd just leave again, or grow resentful and take it out on you." He spoke like it was the simplest of deductions.

"But why would Daddy make me think she was dead?"

"So that you didn't have to know that she was living. Sarah didn't want y'all and your father didn't want you to have to live with that knowledge."

I sat for a moment, trying to process his words. "Where is she now?" I was no longer stunned. Now I was straight pissed off.

"Don't know if your father was in touch with her after that. If so, he never told me. I do know that from time to time, he'd have the private investigator track her down, take a few pics, but as far as I know, he never had contact with her again."

"What is she doing? You don't know where she's living? I need to see her." I had so many questions.

"I wish I could tell you more, baby girl. But that's all I know."

I wanted to scream. How was my daddy able to live this lie and no one knew anything?

I stood, thanked Uncle Clyde, and hugged him before leaving. I still didn't have all the answers but I was more determined than ever to not give up until I did.

CHAPTER 8

There had to be something somewhere. A picture, a letter, some indication of where my mother was. I know Daddy had never stopped loving her, so he had to keep something hidden. I just knew it. The problem was, I wasn't having any luck finding it.

I'd left Uncle Clyde's and waited until I knew my grandmother was in church to come here and go through my father's room.

"Your mother left us long before she left us."

I don't know why the words my father had muttered after an argument when I was sixteen had just popped into my head. I had been too mad about him not letting me go to a party to read into his statement. Now it made perfect sense.

And if he knew she was alive, he had to have something around here that could tell me where she was.

Only, I'd been here for over an hour and had turned up nothing more than an old weathered insurance form with my mother's Social Security number. And that wasn't much help because the last two numbers were worn off.

I tossed a small box off the top shelf of his closet. I had prayed that I would find something in there as soon as my hand felt it in the back. I cried crocodile tears when I opened the box up and only discovered it was full of baby pictures of me. No signs of my mother anywhere.

I was just about to return the box to the shelf when my eyes flickered to a stack of letters tied together. They were under all the photos. I pulled them out and immediately recognized my scraggly little handwriting. All of the envelopes had the same address:

> *To: Mommy*
> *In: Heaven*
> *From: Brooke*

Tears welled as I remembered how for six months straight after my mother's "death," I'd written her letters about how much I missed her. Daddy had told me he'd mailed them and he was sure Mommy was reading them in Heaven.

I sat on the floor to look through the letters. I stopped at an envelope that said:

> *To: Sarah*
> *In: Heaven*
> *From: Brooke*

That had been the very first letter I'd written after my mother died. I remembered it well. And that memory sent my mind racing back to the past.

......

"Something's wrong with Sarah," I told my daddy. We'd just come back from church, which my mother hadn't attended with us because she "didn't feel good." I heard Daddy tell Grandma that she was just being dramatic, but maybe she really was sick because she sat on the sofa, just staring out the window. She didn't answer me and I'd called her name fifteen times.

"What did I tell you about calling her Sarah?" Daddy snapped at me.

"But that's what she wants me to call her," I protested.

"She's your mother. So you call her Mommy."

My mother finally turned her gaze away from the window and glared at my father, like she wanted to say something. I didn't like calling her Sarah, but that's what she always told me to call her.

My mother gripped the coffee cup that was in her hand. "It's okay, Jacob. Really," was all she said.

"No, it's not." He tossed his keys on the counter and removed his suit jacket. "Children don't call adults by their first names, especially their mothers." He turned to me. "Brooke, go to your room."

"But I want to know what's wrong with Sarah," I said. "She looks like she's been crying."

Daddy gently pushed me toward the room. "She's fine. Having an emotional temper tantrum as usual."

......

I'd addressed this letter to "Sarah" in hopes that calling her by her name would make her happy in Heaven. I turned the envelope over, opened it, pulled out the letter, and began reading.

Dear Sarah, please don't be mad but I don't wanna call you by your name any more. I'm sooooo sad. I

miss you. Daddy said you are with God now but can you tell God I still need you so can I have you back? Please? I promise to eat your mashed potatoes if you will just come back to me.

I love you. Brooke.

My name was smeared, as if my teardrops had stained the letter. That caused new teardrops to fall.

I opened another letter. The handwriting was so much more sophisticated and I immediately recognized the little heart at the top as the signature heart I used to do when I was eleven.

I began reading.

Dear Mommy, o.m.g. I got my period today and Mrs. Baker (that's my fourth period teacher) had to tell me what to do. They called Daddy and he had to come pick me up because I messed up my clothes. It was the most embarrassing thing ever! Neither of us said anything all the way home. He stopped, bought me some Maxi pads and told me Grandma would talk to me about it when she got home. I don't want to talk to him or Grandma about this!!! I want to talk to you!!!! I miss you soooo much.

Love, Brooke.

I held the letter close to my heart. That was just one of many times I'd longed for my mother. Grandma was no better than Daddy because it made her uncomfortable to talk about it. All she'd said was, "You can get pregnant now and you'd betta not bring home no babies."

I'd had to get the period basics from Aunt Connie, April's stepmother. She was the same person who gave me the birds-and-the-bees talk, took me to Girl Scouts, and helped me pick out my prom dress. But Aunt Connie suffered from lupus so she was sick a lot and between taking care of April and her own daughter, Mykala, there was only so much she could do for me.

So, I'd done so much alone.

And that memory made me sad.

Then it made me angry.

Emotionally spent, I decided to save the rest of the letters for another time. I needed to keep looking for clues on my mother's whereabouts before my grandmother got home.

I set the stack of letters to the side, climbed back on the ladder, and kept looking in the closet. After fifteen minutes I was no closer to finding anything to help me find my mother.

I slid to the floor as I let out a piercing, frustrated scream, just to release the pent-up stress. From the lie I'd lived. From the pain I felt.

"You 'bout done?"

I looked up to see my grandmother standing in the doorway.

"Now you know Jacob is spinning round and round in his grave at the way you done trashed his room."

I wasn't in the mood for my grandmother. I didn't have the stamina or desire to listen to her lecture. So I just buried my face in my hands and cried.

"Now, now," she said, walking over and extending her hand. She reached down, took my hand, pulled me up, and then led me over to my father's bed.

"Now why are you doing all this? What is it that you're looking for?"

I inhaled, then shot her a sharp look, being careful not to be disrespectful. "Answers. I need answers about my mother. You don't know anything. Uncle Clyde doesn't know anything. It just seems like somebody should know something. I just feel like it's something you're not telling me."

"I told you what I know." She shot daggers my way. "Are you calling me a liar?"

Even in my grief, I knew better than to go there.

"Of course not, Grandma." I sighed. "It's just there has to be something that can give me an idea as to where my mother is."

"Why?" she asked in exasperation. "What are you going to do once you find her?"

"I don't know. Go see her. Talk to her. Ask her why she left me."

"Does it matter why?"

"Of course it does," I cried.

It was her turn to sigh. "I guess I don't understand it."

"Nobody except somebody that has been abandoned can understand it."

"You weren't abandoned." She reached over, pulled me into her plump bosom, and stroked my hair. "You were very much loved by your father and by me, and I know it doesn't seem like it, but your mother loved you, too, in her own way."

"Mothers who love their children don't leave them." I stood and faced my grandmother. My tears were now replaced by anger. "Do you know where she is?"

Her shoulders dropped as she shook her head. "I don't. Your dad knew she was in New York, but he later discovered she'd moved. If your daddy knew where she was he never said a word to anyone. I always thought that he didn't want to know.

Whenever he got a picture, he didn't want to know where it was taken. I think there's a part of him that was scared that if he knew for sure, he'd be inclined to try and go get her and convince her to come back. And he didn't want her anywhere she didn't want to be. He'd been there and done that for too long. Besides, he had crafted this lie, and a lie, once it starts, has to be seen through," she said.

"He didn't have to keep lying to me," I mumbled.

"Well, he did. I won't say that I agreed with it, but I knew how much your daddy loved you. And everything he did, he did for you, to try and make sure you had the best of everything."

"And lying to me was best?" I asked.

"Well, he thought it was and then, when he felt like maybe it wasn't, he was too deep in. Imagine when you were fifteen years old how you would have felt to find out the truth. What it would have done to you. I know that your father didn't want that."

"Your mother left us long before she left us."

I was silent. But if the pain I was feeling now as a grown woman was any indication, I probably wouldn't have been able to handle it as a child.

"So what am I supposed to do now, Grandma?"

She lifted my chin and smiled. "If you have to find her, then you do what you have to do and you make your peace and then you come back to your man and y'all live happily ever after."

My man. I knew Trent was getting irritated with me. He'd been trying to see me since my dad's funeral, but I asked him to give me some time to grieve alone. He hated being shut out, and he was going to be furious when he found out I hadn't told him about my mother. I don't know why I hadn't. I think because I knew he'd have a bunch of questions and the fact that I didn't have answers would only frustrate me even more.

"Trent is so mad at me, but I can't focus on a wedding," I told my grandmother. "I need to find Mama."

"That's understandable." She stood. "And that just means you need to deal with it. Get on that Internet thang y'all do. I saw on *The Ellen DeGeneres Show* the other day somebody found their long-lost mama on that Internet."

I actually had done some searching last night, but there were so many websites. I didn't know where to go or what to trust.

"Go to *The Ellen DeGeneres Show* website. Look on there and see who they use," my grandmother insisted. "It's a start."

"Do you think I'm going to ever find her?" I asked.

"I don't think you'll ever know unless you try. The question you need to be asking is what are you going to do once you do find her?" My grandmother squeezed my arm before leaving me to simmer in her words.

CHAPTER 9

The sight of my fiancé standing at my door with a tiny shih tzu in his hand should have made me smile. Instead all I said was, "A dog? Really, Trent?"

Trent held the dog up to his face and made a puppy dog expression. "I named her Penelope. I figured you needed something to cheer you up." He extended Penelope toward me. I took the white fluffy animal and she immediately nuzzled into my chest. A dog was the last thing I needed.

"See, she likes you." Trent grinned.

I smiled against my will. "A dog, Trent?" I repeated, handing the dog back to him.

He patted the dog on the head, but didn't take her. "I know you've been feeling down," he said, walking into my apartment, "and I just wanted to do something to cheer you up. I hate how you shut me out, but I understand everyone grieves in their own way."

I closed the door with my free hand as Penelope let out a bark. I had been talking about getting a dog for a long time. Both Trent and I really loved pets. And I'd had a beloved

Pomeranian, Diamond, who had died last year. I'd just never been able to bring myself to get a replacement. Eventually, I wouldn't have minded getting a dog, but now was definitely not the time. All of my focus needed to be on finding my mother.

"So," Trent said from the kitchen, "I'm glad you let me come over. I was really worried about you."

He walked back into the living room, a bottled water in his hand.

"I'm good." I set Penelope down and she instantly peed right in the middle of my hardwood floor. I cut my eyes at Trent. "Really?"

He shrugged. "Hey. I didn't say she was house trained."

We both stood staring at the wet spot. I know he didn't expect me to clean it up.

Trent groaned, then grabbed a paper towel to deal with the mess. Penelope darted off to explore her new surroundings.

"I got you a bunch of doggie stuff to go with her. I left it in the car. I'll bring it before I leave." He leaned down, cleaned her mess up, then walked back in the kitchen to put the paper towel in the trash. I heard the water running as he washed his hands. When he returned to the living room, he sat down next to me on the sofa. "So, for real, how are you, babe?"

"Making it." I snuggled into his embrace. "It's gonna be a minute before my heart is right again because you know how close Daddy and I were."

He stroked my hair. "I know."

"But, umm, I have something else I need to talk to you about," I began.

"Me, too," he said.

"You go first," I told him, jumping on any excuse to delay news about my mother, which would be followed by a bunch of questions that I wouldn't have the answers to.

"Well"—he sat up, excitement all over his face—"I need you to keep an open mind and to hear me out before you say no." My eyes locked with his as he continued: "Your father is gone now and your job is flexible so there is nothing keeping you tied here."

"Trent." I raised an eyebrow in anticipation of where this conversation was going.

"No, like I said, hear me out," he continued. "This opportunity to reenlist is huge."

"I don't want to move around from base to base."

"That's the great thing," he said. "I don't have to. I can be based in Norfolk and I'd be in line to be commander of a vessel. Norfolk would be a great place to live, right?"

"Norfolk? A vessel? I . . . my grandmother." I didn't know what to say that wouldn't lead to a fight.

"April is here and she'll keep an eye on your grandmother." He fired off rapid responses like he was ready for my protests. "And we're only four hours away. The worst-case scenario, we'd bring your grandmother with us."

"I don't think so," I said. "If you reenlist, that means at the first sign of trouble, you're gone and I'm left worrying that each call will be someone telling me that you died."

"I could also die walking to the store," he replied. "We can't live our lives in fear."

Trent let out a heavy sigh. He knew all about Jared, so I didn't get why he couldn't understand my fear.

Trent took my hand. "I seriously want you to consider it. This is an amazing opportunity. I can go in on captain status."

A mist covered my eyes and I leaned my head back. I couldn't deal with this right now.

"I'm not moving to Norfolk, Trent," I said.

He dropped my hand. "Why do you always have to be difficult?"

"Because I'm not one of your recruits," I replied, folding my arms in defiance. "I don't follow your orders."

He let out a long sigh, then ran his hands over his head. "Babe, I don't want to fight with you. Just think about it, okay?"

I nodded, my resolve weakening. Anything to end that conversation.

"One other thing," he continued, "and then I'll let you tell me what you wanted to say. I know you didn't really want a big wedding and I'm not saying we need to have some giant wedding like you told me April had, but my mom is just really not feeling the idea of eloping."

"Trent." I sighed.

"That's just something else I want you to consider. We can do something small. You said yourself we don't have money for a giant wedding. But we've been saving and we have enough to do something intimate."

"Okay," I said. I hadn't even thought about what type of ceremony I wanted. "We can talk about it some more later."

That seemed to satisfy him because he kicked back and put his feet up on my coffee table. I popped his knee and he immediately dropped them.

"Sorry, babe. So what did you need to talk to me about?"

I took a deep breath and turned to him. "You remember in the hospital when my dad kept apologizing?"

"Yeah. Did you find out what that was about? Had he been sick and kept it from you?"

I shook my head. "I wish it were that simple. My grand-mother told me he was apologizing for lying to me."

"Mr. Hayes? A liar? Nah," Trent said.

"Yeah," I replied, "and this is one doozy of a lie." Now I had his undivided attention. "Trent, um, he told me that"— I took a deep breath, because this was still difficult to say— "my mother is alive."

"What?" Trent said, his brow furrowing in confusion.

"She isn't dead." Every time I uttered those words it was like I was transported to an alternate universe. My mother had been alive all this time, every time I'd cried for her, during my first date, my prom, going away to college. She didn't have to miss those things. She *chose* to miss those things.

"But, I thought you said she died when you were six or seven."

"That's what they told me," I replied. "We had a funeral and everything. But she didn't die. She ran off."

"Ran off? Who does that? I mean, I heard of men doing it but never a woman."

"Yeah, you and me both. My mother decided she didn't want to be a mother and just up and left."

"Wow." Trent fell back against the sofa, absolutely stunned. "Yeah, that's the last thing I ever expected you to say."

"So now I'm trying to figure out what to do."

He looked confused again. "Figure out what? She ran off. She obviously didn't want to have anything to do with you. I mean," he quickly corrected himself, "I wasn't trying to say it like that, but why would you want to get to know someone that didn't want you?"

"Because she is my mother. I don't know anything about her. I don't know if she's dead or alive since this last picture my grandmother showed me from two years ago. I don't know if she lives here or in Australia or in South America. I need to find out why she left. There has to be a reason. I don't know anything. And I want to know. Maybe she's been looking for me. Maybe we can have a relationship."

He sat in stunned silence before saying, "So, what does that mean?"

"It means I need to find my mother and I won't be able to get any peace until I do."

I was extremely disappointed by the look on Trent's face. I knew that he liked to control things and got all flustered when things weren't "proper and in order," but I couldn't believe I didn't have his unwavering support on this. For the first time since I'd met him, I didn't feel support. And that gave me an ominous feeling inside.

CHAPTER 10

....

*I*t was amazing how far a little forgiveness could go. A year ago, I would've never thought I would be sitting across from my friend Symone ever again. Symone had been part of me and April's crew since high school, but she and I always clashed. April said it was because we were so much alike. Usually we squabbled, then got over it. But last year her boyfriend, Danny, had flirted with me, and Symone got mad at me, despite the fact that I didn't flirt back. Of course, I told her about her insecure self and the end result had been the two of us going our separate ways.

Now, sitting across from her at the restaurant, I was glad that April insisted we meet for lunch. After April got over her initial shock of my mother being alive, she immediately went into action to try to find her and she'd suggested Symone after only a few minutes of thinking.

We'd spent the first hour catching up, and now it was as if we'd never fallen out.

I only agreed to meet with Symone because it had been two weeks since I found out about my mother and I was no closer to finding her than before I knew she was alive. I'd visited every missing-persons website out there, signed up for countless "trials" to gain access to information (I needed to remember to cancel those). And still, nothing. Since Sarah was one of the most common names in the universe, finding her was near impossible.

April was confident that Symone could help me find my mother. And if there was one thing I knew about my former friend, it was, if there was a will for Symone Wiley, there was a way.

"So, now that we've caught up on everything, let's talk about what's really going on in your life," she said. "April filled me in on everything. I'm so sorry." She leaned back, crossing her long, sultry legs. "That has just got to feel awful."

April shot her a look out the side of her eye like she had warned her not to go overboard.

"Yeah, it doesn't feel good," I said, managing a smile. "You know, I'm just trying to find her. April said you might know someone who can help."

"What are you going to do once you find her?" Symone asked what it seemed everyone had been asking.

"I don't know. Get some answers?" I shrugged. "I just need to know if you can help. I mean I don't know how, but if you can . . ."

"Girl, I should have been a private investigator in my other life. Did April tell you about Paul?"

I looked at my cousin, confused.

April shook her head. "No, I don't tell people's business." She smiled at Symone. "You could learn something from that philosophy."

Symone waved her comment off. "Brooke is like family.

You could have told her. Let me tell you about that cheating, no-good, low-down dirty dog that calls himself my fiancé."

She leaned forward and I couldn't help but wonder how this had suddenly become about her, but I let her continue.

"So, I had a feeling in my gut that Paul was up to no good and if it's one thing I try to tell folks, trust your gut. A woman's gut does not lie. So, I just laid low because I know what's done in the dark will come to light. Well, one too many lies didn't add up. Paul was trying to tell me two plus two equals five and I just nodded and was like, 'Okay, you must think I'm one of those ditzy chicks that used to run after you in college.' Well, last weekend I got him good and drunk. Like sloppy, passed-out drunk."

"So, what? You expected him to confess?" I asked, figuring the sooner we could finish her story, the sooner we could get back to my issue.

"Girl, please. No. Because then, of course, when he woke up the next morning he would have sworn he didn't know what I was talking about. So I got him drunk and then when he was out, I got his phone, I took his thumb and put it on the phone so that the thumbprint could unlock his screen."

"Wow," I said, fascinated. "I would have never even thought of that."

"No one should have to do all that," April said, shaking her head.

"Hmph." Symone laughed. "*You* don't have to do all that because you got the last good man on earth. Well, next to Trent, that is." She smiled at me. Symone was always telling me how lucky I was. She went to church with Trent and she said every single woman in the sanctuary wanted him since he was sixteen years old.

"Anyway, as I was saying," she continued. "I started going through his phone and what do I see? Lo and behold, some chick he works with. She was sending him butt-naked pictures on Facebook."

"What? Paul?"

"Yes, Paul, the man I was supposed to marry next year."

"Maybe she didn't know he was in a relationship," I said.

"Hmph, oh she knew all right, because not only did I meet her at the Christmas party last year, but she wanted to make sure I didn't 'have access to his account.' And he told her that I didn't even know about the account. That was mistake number one, because I did know. I was just waiting for the right moment to let him know I knew. Mistake number two, he was so confident I could never get in his phone, he just stays logged in to Facebook. So I was able to see all the pictures and I downloaded each and every one of them."

"Wow, and did what with them?" I asked. Symone had momentarily allowed me to take my mind off my troubles. I was truly engrossed in her story now.

"You're not going to believe this part," April said, leaning back and letting Symone finish the story. "It's all just too much. The girl needs her own reality show."

"I wish you knew how to make it happen," Symone quipped. "Anyway, so I downloaded the pictures, sent them to myself, then I created a new Facebook page for Skeezer-Ho, that's what I named it, Latricia Skeezer-Ho Martin. And I used the naked pictures as her profile pic and all the photos in her album and then I tagged everybody she knew, along with a post detailing her cheating escapades with my fiancé."

"What?" I asked in disbelief.

"Yep. Of course, Facebook ended up taking the page

down, but not before her friends and coworkers got an eyeful. Oh, and I made 'Beware of Lost Dog' flyers and distributed them at her and Paul's job."

"Wow, that's gangster." I smiled.

"Just call me Nino Brown," Symone said, taking a sip of her drink.

"I would never have the guts to do something like that," I said.

"Well, I'll bet the two them will think twice before they mess over the next chick. Sometimes it takes a little payback to make people realize that you don't play."

We laughed some more, which felt really good to be able to do. Still, I really did want to get back on how to find my mother.

"Okay, so back to business," I said. "Can your investigative skills help me figure out how to find my mom?"

"Well, I'm sure you've done all the basics," she said, "like, you know, all the online stuff."

"It's just so much out there that I don't know what to try. I have been looking online but it's turning up nothing. I don't even know what part of the world she's in. She was in New York, but that was at least twenty years ago. I found her Social Security number on an old document. But the last two numbers are worn off so that doesn't even do me any good."

"Well, my cousin is a private eye. I think that PI is in our genes. Do you want me to hook you up with him?"

"Oh, my God. That's exactly what I need," I replied, then quickly thought about the cost. "But I can't afford a private eye." My father had been retired for ten years, so he'd been living on a fixed income. He'd had enough to bury himself, but it wasn't like he'd left me much money. And my grandmother lived in the house, so it's not like I could have sold that, not that I would have anyway. I made a decent living, but not enough to pay a private investigator.

"I'll get him to cut you a deal. He doesn't work for free, but he'll work with you." Symone pulled out her phone and tapped the screen. "If your mother is anywhere in North America, Clint will be able to find her."

I leaned back and took a deep breath. Could it be? Was I really on the way to finding out more about my mother?

"Hey, cousin," she said. "It's Symone. Look, I got somebody that I need you to help out. No, it's not me"—she covered the phone's mouthpiece—"he's talking about he doesn't want to go following Paul again." She returned to the call. "No, it's Brooke, the one I went to school with . . . Yeah, well, we made up. And she needs some help finding her mother. I don't know all the details. I'm going to give her your number so you guys can hook up. You think you can help her? . . . Cool. I'll pass your info on to her."

She hung up the phone and smiled. "My cousin said he's on it. I'll give you his number and you can call and give him any details you have. And if he's on it, it's just a matter of time before he locates her."

She said it with such confidence that for the first time since I'd discovered this tragic news, I had hope. Now I just had to figure out how in the world I was going to get the money to pay for a private investigator.

CHAPTER 11

*T*hree grand. That's how much it would cost me to search for my mother. Symone's cousin had texted me this morning, saying he needed half to get started.

Since I only had about four hundred dollars in my personal savings, I had to take my case to Trent. And our wedding/honeymoon/house fund.

Trent had asked me to meet him for dinner. We'd had a rough and rocky week and I could tell he was hoping we could get back on track. And I was hoping to convince him how important this was to me. I also figured this would be the best time to tell him I needed to pull out some of our money.

But as we sat there at the Olive Garden, I had yet to find the strength to bring it up. The perfect opportunity arose when, after a bunch of small talk, Trent said, "So, any more news on your mom?"

This was the first time he'd asked about it in a week. And that actually stung a little bit. He truly didn't get how important this was to me. Yet he had asked me about moving to Norfolk three times.

"Nothing yet."

Just tell him.

He sighed in frustration, I know from the lack of conversation. Luckily, his cell phone rang. He glanced down at the screen.

"This is my commander. I've been waiting on this call. Excuse me a minute."

He exited the table and I welcomed the reprieve. It gave me time to think. And remember.

• • • • • •

"Mom, I mean, Sarah, are you okay?"

My mother turned away from the window. Her eyes were puffy, like she'd been crying, but she forced a smile. "Hi, Brookie. Yes, I'm fine."

I didn't understand how parents got away with lying. I always got in trouble when I lied.

"What's wrong?"

"Nothing." She walked over and began fluffing my long black ponytails. "How was school today?"

I stood, studying her. Had she really forgotten? "School was fine. But I thought you were coming to my play today."

Her hands went to her mouth in shock. "Oh, no. Sweetie. I forgot. I'm so sorry." She pulled me into a bear hug, as if that would make me forget that she missed me performing as Dorothy in The Wizard of Oz. *I was the first second-grader to land a starring role in the annual school play and my own mother had missed it.*

Before she could say anything else, my father walked in. He'd been happy during my whole performance, but he must have been faking it because on the way home, he was super mad.

"What happened to you? Let me guess," my father said, not giving her time to answer. "Something came up."

"I forgot, but I promise to make it up to you," my mother said. "Matter of fact, go change and I'll take you for ice cream to make up for missing your play."

"It's the middle of the week. You know I don't like her to have sweets during the week. Besides, it's almost seven."

I stuck out my bottom lip. Daddy was always ruining the fun stuff Mommy wanted to do.

Mommy knelt in front of me and took both of my hands. "We'll do something special this weekend," she said. She didn't sound convincing. Still, I nodded and kissed her on the cheek.

I knew that I could get in trouble, but for some reason, I didn't go up to my room. I stood against the wall so I could hear what they were talking about.

"Why must you do this, Sarah?"

"Do what, Jacob?"

"Don't I give you the best of everything?"

"Here we go," she huffed. Mommy was always huffing, like Daddy was getting on her nerves.

"You don't have to work."

"But I want to work."

"You have everything you want."

"What about what I need?" Her voice sounded like it was cracking. "Does that matter at all?"

"Well, Brooke needs you here."

"What about what I need?" she repeated.

I don't know what they said after that because I'd gone up to my room. I just couldn't take the fighting anymore.

······

I'd forgotten how unhappy my mother was. I guess that was one of those things I had blocked out over the years. That had to be why my mother left. But why would she never try to get in touch with me?

"Hello?"

Trent snapped his fingers in front of me. "Oh, sorry. I didn't see you come back," I said.

His frustration was evident. "I feel like you don't see me at all anymore."

"I'm sorry. I just have a lot on my mind," I said.

Trent hesitated, like he was weighing his words. "Brooke, don't take this the wrong way, but do you think you should get some help, maybe go back to the therapist so she can help you through all of this?"

I folded my arms in defiance. "I don't need therapy. I need . . . answers."

He bit into a breadstick, shaking his head as he chewed. "I don't understand. You thought your mom was dead all this time, just keep pretending that she is."

I had to take a moment, because the words that wanted to come out of my mouth were not pretty. I was seeing a side of Trent I did not like.

"I don't expect you to understand," I said. "Your mother didn't walk away from you. You can't even begin to imagine the pain."

"You've been doing just fine all these years." He shrugged.

The callousness of his words pissed me off. "Actually, I haven't been doing fine."

When Trent invited me to dinner, had I known it was going to go down this path, I definitely would have declined. Then I reminded myself of why I did come.

"Look, you know my issues with losing people close to me. But I lost my father, and finding out my mother has been alive all this time makes me feel like I'm losing her all over again. If you can't get that, then I don't know what to tell you."

Trent hated arguing, so I could tell this was draining on him. We sat in silence for a few minutes, both of us toying with our food. Finally, Trent looked at me.

"So where does this leave us?" he asked. "You haven't mentioned the wedding since your father died."

"Good grief, my dad has only been dead three weeks!"

"I know that, but now you've moved on to this quest to find your mother and I'm wondering where that leaves us. Are we still getting married? When? You've shut me out so I'm just in limbo here."

"And we know you can't stand to be in limbo," I mumbled.

"What?" he said.

"Nothing, Trent." I let out a deep sigh. This was all draining on me as well. The day after our engagement, Trent had told me he was moving his savings to a joint account to use for the wedding and our honeymoon and to get our first house. I'd moved half my savings, which wasn't much, but I wanted to contribute since Trent was adamant about beginning our life on solid financial footing. That's why I dreaded what I was about to say.

"Look," I said, deciding to just get it out. "What I do know is I can't give you what you need until I deal with this thing with my mother. Until I find her. I talked to a private investigator. I want to hire him. But it will cost me a three-thousand-dollar retainer, which is really a good deal because normally, it's at least five grand."

Trent looked at me like I had lost my mind. "We don't have

three thousand extra dollars. And a retainer means that's just a starting rate."

I hesitated before saying, "We have the money in our joint savings account." I wasn't even going to address the fact that the fee might go up.

If looks could kill, my fiancé would be Jeffrey Dahmer. "Are you seriously talking about using the money we're supposed to start our life with to track down your mother?" he asked me, his voice a little louder than it should have been.

"That's exactly what I'm saying."

Trent noticed a few people glancing our way, so he leaned forward and lowered his voice. "And do exactly what when you find her?" He didn't give me time to answer as he sat back. "No. You're talking crazy. You don't want me to reenlist, my consulting contract is ending with the agency, and I don't know what our financial situation will be like in a year and you want to blow three grand?"

"It's not blowing," I protested. "Don't you understand I can't get on with my life until I close out this chapter?"

He shook his head, like nothing I said was registering. "So what does that mean?"

"It means, I need that money . . . even if we have to postpone getting married."

The waiter walked over, saw the intensity in our conversation, and slowly eased away.

Trent gritted his teeth. "Are you freaking serious? We have a plan and you want to disrupt it for some wild goose chase?"

"*You* have a plan," I retorted.

He sat back, stunned. "So, now you don't want to get married? This is all me?"

My shoulders sank in frustration. "I didn't say that. I'm just saying that sometimes the best-laid plans need to be flexible. Is that so difficult for you to do?"

He shot daggers in my direction. "Do you know how many women would love to trade places with you?"

It was my turn to return the daggers. "Maybe you need to go find one of them then."

He matched my glare, before saying, "If you postpone the wedding, you might as well call it off."

My frustration turned to shock. This dinner was taking a direction I never would have imagined. "Are you giving me an ultimatum?"

"No, I'm just telling you to think long and hard about what you're doing because I'm not going to have my woman put me on hold while she goes traipsing all over the country, trying to deal with mommy issues."

I stared at him in disbelief. *Who was this man?* "Are you going to grab my hair and drag me back to the cave if I don't obey?" I asked.

My sarcasm was lost on him, because he just threw his fork down and mumbled, "I can't believe this."

I had never seen Trent look at me with such disgust. But right about now, the feeling was mutual. He took out some cash, tossed it on the table, then pushed his chair back from the table as he stood. "I really hope you know what you're doing. And I hope it's worth all you stand to lose."

He didn't say anything else as he headed toward the door.

CHAPTER 12

The light tapping on my office door caused me to look up from my work, which I'd been engrossed in all morning. My assistant, Anita, stuck her head in.

I motioned for her to come in as I nestled the phone between my neck and shoulder. "Again, my sincerest apologies. I'll personally bring the media plan by for you to see this evening," I told my client before hanging up the phone.

I had been screwing up. My boss, Charlene, had given me three weeks off for my father, but while I'd physically returned, mentally I was on my fourth week of leave and my work was suffering because of it.

My job as publicist for one of the largest public-relations agencies on the East Coast was one of the most rewarding things I did. But ever since I'd found out about my mom, it had been nearly impossible to do my job.

"Good morning. You have a package." Anita handed a small brown box to me.

"What is it?" I asked as I took the package from her.

"I have no idea," she replied. "The UPS man just dropped it off."

I slowly opened the small box, wondering if Trent had sent me a gift to make up for our fight. It had been a week, and while we had spoken, it was almost formulaic and tinged with tension.

As soon as I saw the golden locket, I froze. I had forgotten that I had this piece made. It was from an old jewelry set my mother had owned. I had had it melted down and made into a locket.

I pulled the gold chain from the box, not sure whether I should cry or toss it in the trash. When I'd come up with the decision to have this made, I thought I would put my mother's wedding ring on it and put up Jared's ring before saying "I do" to Trent.

"What is it?" Anita asked, peering over my shoulder. "Oh, my God, that's beautiful." She took the locket from me and at that moment, I hated that I treated Anita more like my friend than my assistant.

"Excuse you," I snapped, snatching the necklace away from her.

She stood back, no doubt shocked. "Sorry. I was—"

I took a deep breath. "No, I'm sorry. I didn't mean to snap at you. I just have a lot going on."

She nodded, but I could tell I had hurt her feelings. I made a mental note to really apologize to her later on.

"I'm heading out if there's nothing else." Anita's tone had turned ultraprofessional, which she only did when she was upset with me.

"No, we're good. And Anita, I really am sorry. I'm on edge because, well, it's just been rough with my father's death."

Although I considered her a friend, I wouldn't dare tell her about my mom.

The expression on her face softened. "I understand. See you tomorrow."

As I fingered the necklace, my mind raced back to the original piece of jewelry that had been the origin of this locket.

. . . . . .

"You think you cute."

I shifted my backpack from one shoulder to the next. I swear, I couldn't wait until I graduated. Granted, I was just a junior, but the minute I stepped foot off the grounds of Millbrook High School, I would never return.

I had done nothing to Stacy Sellers, yet here she was, in the middle of the hallway, in my face, going off over some stupid BS.

"Pardon me," I said, stepping around her and trying to get to my third period.

"Pardon me," she said, mocking me. "Look at her, trying to talk white."

I stopped and stared at her. I might have been quiet, but I refused to be intimidated by the resident "mean girl."

"If by white, you mean, proper, then so be it. But I'm not about to do this with you."

"Why not? You too good?" Stacy snapped.

"Because I don't have time for this." I pushed past Stacy and her minions, which I knew she was showing out for.

I had just stepped around her when she reached out and grabbed the necklace off my neck. I stopped, stunned as the chain broke, and the locket my mother had given me for my seventh birthday broke and the heart-shaped pendant bounced on the floor, then rolled into the floor vent.

"Oops." Stacy laughed. "Guess I gotta go to the Dollar Store to replace your necklace."

She turned to her friends and laughed. Before I knew it, I charged her, tackling her like we were in the middle of the Super Bowl.

It had taken three teachers to get me off Stacy. When I was done, she had a black eye, a bruised and busted lip, and a bloody nose. And my pendant—the thing I cherished most from my mother—was gone.

．．．．．．

No one in high school messed with me after that. In fact, people gossiped that I was crazy. That had been just fine with me.

My ringing cell phone pushed away thoughts of those brutal high school years.

I picked the phone up off my desk, and despite the unknown number, I answered.

"Hello."

"Hey, is this Brooke?"

"May I ask who's calling?"

"It's Clint."

My heart skipped a beat at the sound of the private investigator's voice. After I sent his deposit via the Cash App, he'd told me he'd only call if he had something. And since it had been less than two weeks since I gave him the deposit, I wasn't expecting him to have found out anything yet.

"Hi, Clint," I said.

"I got something. Can you meet?"

"Yes." My voice was barely above a whisper and the phone trembled in my hand.

"Cool. Can you meet me at that Starbucks on the corner by your job?"

I immediately stood and started gathering my things. "Wait, how do you know where I work?"

He laughed. "I'm a private investigator, remember?"

"Okay." Any other time, I might have laughed with him, but my nerves were on edge. "I'll be there in fifteen minutes."

I hung up and pressed the speaker on my desk phone. "Hey, Anita, I have to step out for a minute. If Charlene comes can you let her know that I'll be back?"

"I got you covered," Anita replied. Charlene was the vice president of First Impressions Public Relations, and my boss. She was great at what she did but she was also a micromanager who was apt to dip into my office at any time of the day.

I grabbed my purse and made a beeline for the door. Fifteen minutes later I was sitting at a table in front of Starbucks, drilling my fingers on the hardwood table and wondering how this information I was about to receive would alter the course of my future.

Clint rolled in like he'd just stepped off the set of a Hollywood movie. He wore dark sunglasses and a long, leather coat, looking like a combination of Shaft and Barack Obama. The coffee shop was packed, yet he headed straight over to me.

"Brooke?"

"Yes."

"Dang, anybody ever told you that you look like that actress Sanaa Lathan?"

I nodded. "All the time."

"Well, you two could be sisters." He didn't remove his shades as he slid into the seat across from me and passed an envelope across the table. "Anyway, here you go."

"Is this what I think it is?" I asked.

"It's what you hoped it would be," he replied, his face stoic.

"Wow, that was fast." I took the envelope and just held it in my hands.

"Didn't Symone tell you that I'm good at what I do? And it really wasn't that hard."

"So . . ." I fingered the envelope, fear keeping me from ripping it open.

"Everything is in there," he said.

I finally picked up the envelope and it trembled in my hand.

"I almost feel guilty about charging you," Clint said. "This was one of the easiest cases I've had, especially with that partial Social."

I finally got the courage to unfasten the large manila flap. I pulled out his report and started reading. Sarah Hayes was now Sarah Ford, an elementary school principal in Atlanta. I scanned the report. It had her home and work address. Paperclipped to the report was an 8x10 picture of her standing in front of the school. She looked exactly like the picture my grandmother had given me.

"That pic is from three days ago. Took it myself."

"So, she's working with kids?" I asked.

He nodded. "Seems that way."

"Do you know any personal information? I mean, besides her address."

He motioned to another piece of paper in the envelope. I pulled it out. It was a photocopy of an article from an Atlanta newspaper. I read the headline: COUNCILMAN ANTHONY FORD TIES THE KNOT.

"So she's married?" I don't know why I had immediately assumed she was living under an alias.

"Yep. But that's all I know." He pointed to the report. "I didn't know how far you wanted me to dig. You said just find her, so I don't have any other details. I can get more, but it'll cost you."

"Wow. Just like that, huh? She wasn't even in hiding or anything." I think I was still in shock. I wasn't prepared to deal with this so soon.

Clint shrugged. "Like I said, it was easy. You just gotta know where to look."

"I don't believe she's this close." I stared at the report. "Thank you," I finally said.

"No problem." He paused. "And like I said, I *almost* feel bad. But I spent a week in Atlanta, so I'm gonna need the rest of my money." I expected him to smile. He didn't.

"Of course," I mumbled, reaching in my purse and pulling out my checkbook.

He raised an eyebrow. "I don't take checks."

"But I don't carry that much cash with me." I had been so excited to meet with him, I hadn't even thought to run by the bank to get his other fifteen hundred.

Clint tsked his irritation. "Fine. Since you're Symone's friend, I guess you're good for it. Make it out to Clint Young."

I scribbled on the check, tore it out, then handed it to him.

"Can I go cash this right now?" he asked.

"Yes, definitely." A part of me felt sad. I'd used our money for something he made it seem like, if only I'd been a little more patient, I could have found myself.

"Cool." Clint stood. "I usually don't ask this, because it really ain't my business. But what do you plan to do with the information?"

I hesitated because I really didn't have an answer. "Not sure yet."

"My dad abandoned me when I was little. By the time I

found him he was dead. I always wondered what it would've been like to reunite with him. That's the only reason I asked."

"I'll let you know." I held the report to my chest. "But thank you again. You have no idea how this helped."

He finally smiled. The look on his face told me he really was happy to help.

"Take care," he said, heading out of the coffee shop.

I stared at my mother's picture. "We'll meet soon," I mumbled. "I promise you that."

CHAPTER 13

I paced back and forth across my apartment, trying to figure out what I was going to do, how and when I would go meet my mother. April was stretched out across my sofa, her feet propped up on my designer throw pillows.

I'd left my meeting with Clint, called April, and told her to meet me at my place. She'd actually beat me there and was waiting, kicked back on my sofa, by the time I arrived.

"I just can't believe she's been living this close all this time," I said. I had so many questions. Did my mother just block me out of her mind? Had she ever tried to see me? How could she just go on like I didn't exist? "I want to go down there," I continued. "I want to see this woman face-to-face. I've got to talk to her."

"Okay, so go to Atlanta," April replied as she finished reading the article about my mother and her husband's wedding.

I know my emotions were in overdrive because my instincts had been to just keep going down I-85 to Atlanta after I left Clint. Thankfully, common sense had set in.

"The problem is I've already been off three weeks. I don't

know how long I would need to be there. And what do I do when I see my mother? Just walk up and say, 'Hey, remember me?'" I plopped down next to my cousin and buried my head in my hands.

"You gotta go or you're gonna drive yourself crazy," April said. "You could always call in sick."

"I can't do that. First of all, I don't want to leave them out there like that. Secondly, my clients need me. I've already been slacking off on them."

"You're already on the verge of losing your man behind this. If you don't do something, you're going to drive yourself— and me—insane and push him even further away. You know where Aunt Sarah is, you have to go see her. You have to see it all the way through now."

On the verge of losing my man. That hurt my heart. I shook away that thought. I wasn't going to lose Trent. We were just in a bad place right now. As soon as I got all this worked out with my mother, he and I would get back on the right track.

"It's just so foul what Aunt Sarah did," April continued. "I'm pissed and she was just my aunt, so I know you're livid."

"I know, right?"

"She better be lucky Mama isn't around," April added. "Because Josephine did not play when it came to her baby brother."

I didn't remember much about my aunt Jo, but I knew she loved my daddy something fierce.

"Do you think she knew my mother was alive?"

April shrugged. "I don't know. I can't see mama letting Uncle Jacob get away with a secret like that."

I still hadn't reconciled my father's deception. One day, I'd have to make peace with that, to try to understand my daddy's motives. But right now, my concentration was on coming face-to-face with my mother.

"So, what's the game plan?" April asked. "Maybe if you figure that out, we can work from there."

I released a heavy sigh. "I don't know what to do. I definitely want to go down there, I *need* to go down there. But I can't be away from work that long."

April bolted upright as a thought came to her. "Wait a minute. Didn't you tell me you guys have an Atlanta office?"

"Yeah, we do. And?"

"You can't work out of there?"

I had never even thought about that. And the Atlanta office had just lost its lead publicist and was severely understaffed.

April grinned like she had just figured it all out. "I think you need to come clean with your boss. Tell her what's going on. Your clients are all over the country anyway. It's not like you need to be local. Tell her they have to let you work from Atlanta or you're quitting."

"I cannot quit my job," I said.

"You're not going to have to. They are not about to lose you. You just snagged Len, that rapper. They're claiming he'll be the next Kanye. With less drama. He's huge."

She was right about that. I was proud of that get. I wasn't into rap royalty, but I'd met Len's sister at an event and she was impressed with me and introduced me to Len. Within a week, they were hiring our agency.

"So they're not going to fire you," April declared. "Or better yet, tell her you're trying to get Tyler Perry as a client."

"So you want me to lie?"

April threw up her hands in exasperation. "Okay, so don't lie. When you get down there, call Tyler and see if he wants to hire you. He'll say no since he does everything himself and you can tell your boss you tried." She leaned back on the sofa, crossed her arms over her protruding belly, and smiled. "Problem solved."

I finally managed a smile. But I loved that about April. She didn't wallow in problems. She was always about solutions, making things happen. That was a quality I definitely needed to emulate.

"So, I'm going to Atlanta?" I said, the thought actively registering.

"You're going to Atlanta. Now, you just need to figure out what you're going to do once you get there."

That was the million-dollar question. And I planned to figure it out sooner rather than later.

CHAPTER 14

I was going to Atlanta.

Charlene had jumped at the idea of me temporarily relocating there until they found another lead publicist. So one day after my request, I was on my way.

But first, I had some crucial business to take care of.

Penelope wiggled in my arms and tried to lick my face. I loved my dog, but not that much, so I set her down on Trent's floor and hoped that she didn't pee on his white shag rug.

I'd brought Penelope to him today to hopefully ease the tension of the news I was about to deliver.

"So . . . I know you're not really feeling my search for my mother."

"It's not that," Trent said, cutting me off. He leaned down to pet Penelope, who was yipping at his leg. "You know I want you to be happy. But I don't want you to forget about the life we were building, either."

"We're still building a life," I said.

"Of course I know that. I mean, I was mad the other day." He stood, walked over, then pulled me close to him. "But you're about to be my wife. I'm not going to lose you over this."

His words sent a ripple of relief through my body. Ever since my father died, we'd been fighting like never before. Despite our problems, I didn't want to lose Trent. I'd sent him several love texts this morning telling him as much. I just hoped what I was about to say didn't take us back down that rocky road.

"Good." I leaned in and kissed him. "Because I need you to be understanding a little while longer because I'm temporarily relocating to Atlanta."

He dropped his arms from around my waist and took a step back. "Excuse me?"

I bit my bottom lip, then said a silent prayer for him not to flip out. "I found my mother."

"What?" he exclaimed. "When? Where?"

"Clint actually tracked her down in Atlanta."

He paused, his brow scrunched up. "Who is Clint?"

"The private investigator."

A silence hung over us before Trent said, "So you hired him?"

I didn't respond.

"Did you take the money out of our savings?"

"I told you that I was going to hire him. You know I was going to use the money."

Trent exploded. "Are you freaking kidding me?" His outburst sent Penelope scurrying under the sofa. "I knew you talked about wanting to use the money. So you just went and withdrew the money without talking to me?"

"I did talk to you." I tried to keep my voice steady so he didn't get even more worked up.

"But we didn't come to any concrete decisions."

I did, I wanted to remind him, but I figured now wasn't the time.

Anger pierced his steps as he paced his living room. "So you took our money and now you're telling me you're moving to Atlanta? For how long?"

"Just for a couple of months. I'm helping them out at the Atlanta office until they get someone in to lead it. And that will give me a chance to reestablish my relationship with my mother."

"If she wanted a relationship with you, don't you think she would've gotten in touch with you?" he snapped.

His piercing words pierced my heart. But he didn't seem to notice as he created a worn path in the shag carpet, ranting unlike anything I had ever seen. I sat on the love seat, tuned him out, and started planning when I would leave.

It wasn't until he said, "I truly don't understand this absurd obsession with your mother," that I turned my focus back to him.

"My obsession? That's what you think this is?"

I guess the fury in my eyes told him that he'd crossed a line because he snapped, "I didn't mean it like that."

"No, you meant it exactly like you said it."

Penelope came from under the sofa, staring as we went back and forth.

"All I'm saying is you took the money that we were saving to start our life. And you think that's okay?"

"It was my money, too."

"Yes, it was *our* money. We saved for a specific reason and you take it and blow it on a private investigator."

"I didn't *blow* it on anyone. I hired someone with it. I did what I had to do." My voice was cracking. I needed support, not resistance.

"And screw everyone else in the process," he said.

We stared at one another, neither of us saying a word. Finally, I just said, "I'm sorry you don't understand."

Truthfully, it didn't surprise me that he didn't get it. Mrs. Grant was there doting on him his whole life. I don't know why my mother left, but it had to be a compelling reason. And I was excited about the prospect of rekindling our relationship. Whatever issues she had twenty-five years ago had to be gone. And if they weren't, we would just work through them.

Of course, I worried about her still wanting nothing to do with me. But I was channeling my inner Oprah and focusing on an optimistic outcome.

And the man I loved was the biggest obstacle to reuniting with my mother.

A knock on the door interrupted our conversation. Trent huffed as he stomped over to open the door. Kimala and Mrs. Grant bounced in. Two of Kimala's kids raced past me. The oldest, a sixteen-year-old, went to Trent's bedroom, barely uttering hello. Demarcus went straight for Penelope, who darted underneath the sofa. He immediately began pulling her leg trying to get her out. I didn't blame Penelope. I wish that I could disappear, too.

"Hello, my beautiful son and daughter-in-law," Mrs. Grant said, walking in and dropping two shopping bags on the floor. It looked like an assortment of flowers in the bags. "I didn't know you'd be here, Brooke. But that works out wonderfully. I brought some floral displays to look at for the wedding."

His mother didn't seem to notice the tension in the room as she dug in the bag and pulled out a stack of magazines.

"I was also thinking we could look through these and find you a dress. I think we should do a March wedding. That gives us enough time to plan. You will make an amazing spring bride."

"Uh, Mama," Kimala said, looking back and forth between me and her brother. I hadn't moved from my spot on the love seat and Trent was standing by the front door, his cheeks puffed out, his arms folded across his chest. "There might not be a wedding."

Her mother finally noticed me. "Are you crying, Brooke?"

I glanced at my reflection in the mirror that hung over his sofa. I didn't even realize my eyes were red and puffy.

"Trent, is it going to be a wedding?" Kimala asked, studying her brother even harder.

"I don't know," he said, never taking his eyes off me.

Mrs. Grant spun toward him. "What do you mean, you don't know?"

I couldn't help but stare, too. "Yeah, what do you mean, you don't know?"

The anger in his voice was evident. "Obviously, her priorities aren't with me."

"And I never realized how selfish you were," I retorted.

"Ooooh," Kimala said as she plopped down on the sofa.

"Is Uncle Trent and Brooke fighting?" Demarcus stopped trying to maul my dog and looked up at us.

Of course, I expected someone to tell him to stay out of grown folks' business, but Kimala simply said, "Yeah, baby, sit down so we can watch."

Both Trent and his mother shot her an evil look, but she didn't seem fazed.

Mrs. Grant took my hand, pulled me up, then walked over

and took Trent's hand. "Look, I know planning a wedding can be stressful."

"She's leaving," he said, cutting his mother off.

"What?"

"I'm not leaving. I'm just temporarily moving."

Trent and I never took our eyes off one another as his mother held our hands.

"I don't want a long-distance relationship," he said matter-of-factly.

I turned to his mother, trying to get her to understand. "The lead publicist in our Atlanta office took a job in Miami, so they needed someone to run the office for a while. So, I'm just going to work in my company's Atlanta office for a while. And Atlanta is not long distance. It's six hours away."

"Why would you do something like that?" his mother asked, releasing my hand. "You're planning a wedding, about to start a family, and you're just going to up and leave?"

I exhaled. "I have something I need to go take care of."

"She wants to go find the mother who abandoned her."

I glared at Trent. I couldn't believe he'd told my business like that, and so callously.

"Abandoned? I thought your mama was dead?" Kimala said, jumping up.

Trent must have known he'd said too much because he closed his mouth and turned away.

"Someone want to tell us what's going on?" Kimala said when neither of us responded.

"Trent, what's going on?" his mother repeated.

"Yeah, Trent," I said, gathering my things. "Why don't you tell your family my whole sordid story." I motioned for Penelope to come, which she immediately did, grateful for the escape from Demarcus. I nuzzled her to me. "Mommy will be back. Daddy is gonna take good care of you." Penelope barked. I petted her head, set her down, and turned to Trent. "I'll talk to you later. Goodbye, Mrs. Grant, Kimala."

With that, I left Trent and his family. I had a sinking feeling that this whole conversation was the beginning of the end.

CHAPTER 15

$\mathcal{I}$ couldn't shake this funk, and that disaster at Trent's place yesterday hadn't made things any better. But I had to push that aside and focus on doing what I needed to do—going to face my mother.

My emotions ran the gamut.

One minute, I envisioned my mother bursting into tears at the sight of me as she pulled me into her arms and begged for my forgiveness. The next, I was seeing her asking why I'd come back into her life, since it was obvious she wanted nothing to do with me.

I couldn't wait to see which scenario was going to play out. I'd gotten everything lined up. My old college roommate, Tammy, was an actress with a place in Atlanta. Since she was in Australia shooting a movie for six weeks, she'd said that I would be more than welcome to stay at her place. I just had to swing by her cousin's house and pick up the key.

Everything was set, my car was loaded up. I just needed to tell my grandmother what was going on, then hit the highway to Atlanta. I smiled as I thought of how I was chasing my dream—reuniting with my mother—and a memory that I'd long ago forgotten resurfaced.

· · · · · ·

"I need to go, Jacob. Why is that so hard for you to understand?"

"Oh, that's right. You need to dance," Daddy said. He sounded like he did when he was fussing at me. *"Give me a break, Sarah. You have a family."*

"That's why I told you I wanted to wait, why I didn't want a family yet. There was so much I wanted to do."

"Well, life doesn't always work out like we want it to, now does it? That's part of being a grown-up. You adjust and do what you have to do."

"And you just forget what you want to do, huh?"

He let out a long sigh. "I even offered to help you open a dance school."

"I don't want to open a dance school. I want to dance."

"Oh, I'm sorry, did Juilliard call?"

"No, but M. C. Hammer did."

My eyes widened. M. C. Hammer called my mama?

"Do you hear how ridiculous you sound?" my father snapped. "I don't even know why you auditioned for that mess. You want to leave your family to be one of nine hundred backup dancers for M. C. Hammer? That is the most asinine thing I've ever heard. Besides, I asked you to make a choice—decide what you wanted—and you said you wanted me. You wanted us."

"Why can't I have it all? I want it all," she cried.

"That's the problem, you don't know what you want. I give you

everything. Am I abusive? Verbally? Physically? No. None of that. All I do is work and try to love you and it's never good enough."

Daddy was getting even madder than he was when Mommy missed the play.

"Just forget it," Mommy replied. "You're right. I'm being ungrateful. I'm sorry. I'm going out to get some fresh air."

I peeked around the corner to see the front door slam as my mother left. My grandmother came down the stairs and I ducked back behind the staircase.

"I don't know how you do it," she said.

"Mom, please don't start."

"That girl is the most ungrateful thing I've ever seen. You picked her up out of the gutter. Gave her all of this. And she acts like you're holding her prisoner."

I made a note to use the dictionary Grandma had given me for Christmas to find out what gutter meant.

"If she wants out, let her go," my grandmother continued. "Find you another one of her."

"Don't be ridiculous, Mother. I'm not breaking up my family."

"Hmph."

Uh-oh. My leg was falling asleep. I carefully tried to shake it to get rid of the cramp that was coming on. But my head hit the staircase and there was a large thud.

"Is that you, Brooke?" I could hear my grandmother's footsteps coming my way. "Somebody has some rabbit ears. Hasn't your mama told you about eavesdropping on folks? My fault, your mama probably ain't told you nothing," she murmured.

"Mother," Daddy said, appearing on the side of her.

She threw her hands up as I crawled from my hiding spot.

"I wasn't eavesdropping," I protested.

"Don't fix your lips to lie to me, girl," my grandmother said.

"Were you eavesdropping, baby?" Daddy asked.

I slowly nodded. "I'm sorry. I was just trying to find out why Mommy was sad."

My grandma and Daddy exchanged looks. I thought I was in big trouble, but Daddy just said, "Just make sure you don't do that again."

"Hmph." My grandmother turned and stormed back up the stairs.

"Mommy is fine," Daddy said. "She went out to get some air. You go run up and take your bath, then come back down for dinner."

I did as he said, grateful to escape without getting into too much trouble.

. . . .

It just dawned on me, that was the last time I'd seen my mother. Her "car accident" happened that same day.

That was the day that the lie that had become my life had begun.

"Hi," I said, walking into the living room at my grandmother's house. I don't know how Grandma stayed here. My father's presence was everywhere. His bowling medals, his photos, even his fishing gear, which still sat in the corner.

"So, that's how you greet me? No hug, no love, just an ol' dry hi?" My grandmother was sitting in her rocking recliner watching *Family Feud*. But she picked up the remote and muted the show.

Since my father died, I came to check on her almost daily. I wanted her to move out of the house and into an assisted living facility, but anytime I brought it up, she wasn't trying to hear it.

I was silent for a few minutes, then said, "I found out where my mother is."

"What?" my grandmother exclaimed.

"She's living in Atlanta," I continued. "She got a new last name. Built a new life. But she's right down the road. She's been there for years."

My grandmother's hand went to her chest. "My Lord."

"I'm going to Atlanta," I proclaimed.

"And do what, baby?"

I shrugged. "I don't know. Confront her, get answers, reunite with her. I just know I have to do something. This is consuming me. I'm not going to be able to do anything until I see her. So, I'm gonna be gone a little while. I'll be working out of the Atlanta office."

"Wait. So you're moving there?"

"I'm just temporarily relocating. My boss needs me to help out there until they get someone there permanently. I'll use that time to hopefully rebuild things with my mom."

My grandmother shook her head. "I don't understand why the need to do all of that. Why can't you just go down there, see her, and come on back?"

"I haven't worked all of that out. I just need to be able to get away. And the only way to get my boss on board is to agree to work from the office there."

"Are you hoping that your mother will see you, then you guys can reconnect?" she asked.

I'd be lying if I said a part of me didn't desperately want that. "I don't know. I just know that I'm allowing myself some time. Plus, with everything going on with Trent . . ." I let my words trail off so I didn't cry.

My grandmother lifted my chin so that I was looking directly at her. "What's going on with Trent?"

I swallowed the lump in my throat. "I think we may have

broken up. He's not too happy about me leaving. I hate to do this to him. But I just can't. Getting married is the last thing on my mind right now. And he's gung ho on doing that. He's focused on building a life. How can I concentrate on that when the mother I thought was dead is alive? For all I know, she's been waiting to reunite with me."

"Waiting, huh?" my grandmother replied. I expected her to launch into a sarcastic tirade but instead she just nodded her understanding. "Well, I guess if there's a roadblock on your path to happiness, you have to stop and move it out of the way."

That made me smile.

"And who knows. It's been a long time. Hopefully, your mama is a different woman now."

Of course, I still had a thousand questions, but suddenly I had a thought. "Wouldn't it be great if my mom could be at my wedding?"

"If that would make you happy, then I hope it happens." She patted my hand. "You do what you have to do."

The fact that my grandmother had given me her blessing made me feel so much better. And my optimism had gone up a notch. Not only was I going to rekindle my relationship with my mother, but it would make my world complete if she were there on my wedding day.

The thought made me anxious to get on the road to Atlanta.

CHAPTER 16

I'd never been one to harbor any hate in my heart, but right about now, I could give the Klan a run for their money with the level of hate running through my body.

I'd finally found my mother.

She wasn't destitute or delusional. She looked . . . happy.

I'd arrived in Atlanta two hours ago and instead of going to get settled, I typed my mother's address, which I'd gotten from Clint's report, into the GPS and came straight here. And I'd been sitting here for two hours, my anger growing with each passing moment.

I'd been filled with joyful anticipation on the drive here. Now what I was feeling—the contempt, the outrage—was in a whole different stratosphere as I watched my mother pull bags from the trunk of a Mercedes. A little girl with long plaits jumped out of the car and bounced around to help her.

They had just pulled up, oblivious to my car parked across the street. My mother was looking like she was in a scene straight out of *Leave It to Beaver*. Domesticated. Content, like she'd just completely forgotten that she'd had a whole other life. That she had a daughter. Had she erased me from her memory? *How* could she erase me from her memory?

I had yet to have children but I could never imagine just walking away from them. I don't know why, but images of Mrs. Grant, her bickering kids, and her unyielding love for them flashed through my mind. I bet she would've never left any of her children.

I fought back the stinging tears. I don't know what I expected, but deep down, I had hoped to find my mother incapacitated, confined to a wheelchair even, unable to talk. Maybe that would explain everything. Because this explained nothing. In fact, it opened the door to more questions.

······

"I wanted to go shopping with you."

The tears were streaming down my face as my mother waltzed in with a handful of bags. I'd been sitting by the window, waiting on her to get home for the past three hours.

"You said last night that I could go," I cried.

"Awww, sweetie, you were asleep and I didn't want to bother you," she said as she set her bags on the sofa.

"Hmph."

My grandmother's huffing caused both of our attention to turn to her. She was standing in the entryway from the dining room. She'd been in and out of the living room trying to console me since I'd awakened to find my mother gone this morning.

"More like you didn't want to be bothered," my grandmother mumbled before disappearing back into the kitchen.

······

I had no memories of shopping with my mother. I only recalled that one of *wanting* to shop with her.

So this sight infuriated me.

My mother kissed the little girl on the head and handed her a bag. Oh, how I wished I could hear their conversation. I started to get out, stomp out, and bust up her perfect little picture. In fact, I had just reached for my driver's-side door handle when my cell phone rang.

I looked down to see April's number and contemplated not answering. But she'd been blowing my phone up since I crossed the Atlanta city limits.

"Did you find her?" she asked as soon as I said "Hello."

"I did." I glared in my mother's direction as some man opened the door for them to enter the house. "She's living the perfect little life."

"Wow," April said. "What did she say when you told her who you were? I knew I should've come."

"I haven't approached her yet. I'm parked outside of her house, watching her."

"Watching her?" April replied. "For what? When are you going to go introduce yourself?"

"I don't know. I thought it would be the first thing I did, but I guess . . . I don't know. I just wasn't expecting this. I guess I hadn't thought this all the way through." The sick feeling in my gut intensified.

"Well, why are you just sitting in the car? You wanted some answers. The only way you're going to get them is to go talk to her."

The front door opened and my mother and the little girl came out and got back in the car. The man was with them. "Wait, they're leaving. It's Sarah, some man, and a little girl."

"A little girl?" April sounded like she was in the middle of a suspenseful movie waiting to find out what happened next. "Who is she?"

"I told you, I don't know anything yet."

They started backing out of the driveway, so I put April on speakerphone, started my car, threw it into drive, and followed them.

"What are they doing now?" April asked.

"They're going somewhere and I'm following them."

"Following them? Where?"

"I don't know," I snapped, weaving in and out of traffic trying to catch up to them. A driver I'd just cut off blared his horn and shot me the middle finger.

"Screw you, too!" I yelled. I was shaking because I didn't know what I was doing. Why was I following them?

"Brooke, maybe this isn't such a good idea," April said, her voice full of apprehension.

"Do you think the little girl is hers?" I asked.

"Maybe she's babysitting." April's tone was hushed, like she was privy to some big secret. "I don't know."

I thought about the loving way Sarah had stroked that little girl's hair before handing her the shopping bag. That was . . . a mother's love. The thought made me sick from the inside.

Silence filled the car as I exited the freeway. They were three cars in front of me.

"Maybe this isn't a good idea," April repeated. "Maybe you should come home and rethink this plan and we figure out what we're going to do."

"No. I'm here now. And I'm not leaving Atlanta until I confront her." I silently noted how now, instead of planning to *see* her, I was preparing to *confront* her. "Besides, it's only going to take a minute for me to get things set up in the Atlanta office, so I have a little time. I just need to figure some stuff out."

I followed them a few more blocks until they pulled in front of an ice cream shop called Jubilee.

"They're parking. So let me call you later," I said.

April let out a long sigh. "Be careful, okay? I love you."

"I will. And I love you back."

I hung up the phone and parked a couple of cars down. I got out and slipped on my shades. At least my mother was consistent with the need to give kids sweets. Getting ice cream was one of the things she used to love doing with me.

The little girl bounced with delight as my mother and the man each took one of her hands. They looked so happy. Something I couldn't recall her ever being with my father. I lingered back before following them inside.

Maybe she is the babysitter, I told myself. Or better yet, maybe it was the man's daughter and my mom was just playing stepmom. Although that still stung, I could process that much better than the idea that Sarah had basically written me off and given birth to my replacement.

"Please Mommy and Daddy, can I have sprinkles on my ice cream?" the little girl said once they approached the counter.

Mommy. I almost lost my balance. I held on to the counter to steady myself, then grabbed a menu when a couple of people looked my way.

"Yes, you may," my mother replied. "And since you did so well at piano lessons this morning, let's make it two scoops with sprinkles!"

Piano lessons, trips to the ice cream parlor. They were just the regular all-American family. While her real family—

while *I* was hundreds of miles away, grieving her. The thought pissed me off all over again.

"May I help you?"

I jumped at the sound of the server's voice. "Not yet, still deciding."

I peeked over the menu as my mother and her family laughed, picked up their orders, and then went and took a seat over in the corner. I ordered a plain vanilla ice cream cone, then sat at the table behind them with my back to my mother. It was crazy, but I wondered if she could feel my presence. Didn't motherhood give you some kind of telepathic connection?

After a few minutes of frivolous conversation, the door to the ice cream shop opened and a handsome young man walked inside. With a head full of curly hair and deep dimples, he was a younger replica of the man sitting across from my mother. I didn't even realize it, but my eyes followed him until I was all but turned around in my seat. I quickly composed myself and shifted my body so I wasn't so blatantly obvious.

"What's up?" he said, pulling out a chair at their table and plopping down in it.

"Hello, son," the man replied. "Glad you could take time out of your busy day to spend a few minutes with your family."

"I'm at work. I could barely break away," he said, scooting the chair closer to their table. He dipped a finger in the little girl's ice cream.

"Ewww," she squealed as they all laughed.

"Well, we're glad you made time," my mother said, patting his cheek. *Could that be her son?* I immediately started doing calculations in my head. He had to be about twenty-five.

Maybe that's why she left. She was pregnant and it wasn't my father's child. Still, how could she have left me behind?

I continued toying around with my ice cream, trying to keep my eavesdropping as inconspicuous as possible. After twenty minutes, they all rose to leave. I contemplated which one I should follow. I quickly assessed that I wasn't about to confront my mother in front of her husband and daughter so I needed to follow the young man.

Coward!

I pushed away that little voice that was ready to fuel my fire and feed into the anger that was consuming me. No, I told myself. I wasn't scared, well, not much. It's just that I decided I would get more answers from the young man.

I followed him into Barnes & Noble, which was two doors down from the ice cream shop.

I browsed until I saw him put on a blue apron, grab a box of books, and head to the science fiction section.

I took a deep breath and approached him. "Hi, can you give me a recommendation for a good book?" I asked.

His dimples greeted me before he did. "I sure can." He set the box down. "Depends on what you like to read. No, wait, let me guess." He cocked his head like he was studying me. "You strike me as a fiction reader, but not some sappy romance." He snapped his fingers. "I know, you like erotica." He flashed a mischievous grin.

I pushed my anger at my mother back and summoned my inner flirt. Of course, that would be completely disgusting if he turned out to be my brother, but I didn't know how else to find out. "You had me pegged right the first time. Just simple contemporary fiction."

"You want something lighter or classics. I highly recommend one of my faves, Lolita Files's *Child of God.* Or if you want something more militant, there's Dwayne Smith's *Forty Acres.*"

"I'll try *Child of God,* that sounds interesting."

"Follow me." He headed over two rows. "It's an older book and usually the stores don't stock older titles but since this is a personal fave, I make sure it stays on the shelves."

I was impressed with his book knowledge.

He went straight to the book and pulled it off the shelf. "You're gonna love it," he said, handing it to me.

I took the book. "Thanks, ummm . . ." I leaned over to look for his name tag. "Alex."

"Yep, I'm Alex. And what's your name?"

"I'm Mona," I replied. "Did I just see you next door at the ice cream shop?"

"Oh, yeah, I was just in there. I ran in to see my peeps."

"I think I was leaving when you were coming in. Your mother sure is beautiful," I said. I hoped I wasn't being too obvious but I needed to see what I could find out.

"Thanks, but that's my stepmom. My mom died when I was little."

Relief swept through my body. "Oh. I'm sorry. I just assumed because she looks just like that little girl."

"My sister, Sunny." He flashed a proud big-brother smile. "That is her daughter."

Her daughter. The sick feeling inside me intensified and once again, I was about to lose my balance. "Well, thank you for your help. I can't wait to dive into this book."

"I'm here to serve."

I didn't know what my plan was but I knew I needed to keep Alex close. I stopped just as I was about to turn. "Ummm, you wouldn't happen to know of any book clubs in the area, would you? I'm new here and I'd love to meet up and talk with someone about the book."

He hesitated, then said, "Uhhh, I'm someone."

I smiled. That was too easy. "Well, give me your number. Maybe we can grab coffee and chat about the book once I'm done."

His eyes grew wide. "Wow. Yes. I'd love that. I'm sorry, I would've asked for your number but I just assumed a woman like you was taken."

"No, I'm very much single." I smiled again. "But it's just coffee."

He grinned like a child who'd just been caught sneaking cookies. "Right. Just coffee and a good book discussion."

And all the information I can gather, I thought as I handed him my phone to put his number in.

CHAPTER 17

$\mathscr{I}$'d turned into a stalker. For the past five days, I'd stalked my mother every day. I followed her to the grocery store. To work. To the gym. Five days. I'd halfheartedly worked. I'm sure Charlene was livid because I'd been giving her excuses but no results. But I just hadn't been able to function. I was consumed with learning all I could about my mother.

Maybe Trent was right. I'd become obsessed. I wanted to understand Sarah. I wanted to see what was it about this life that made her want to forget her other life. What made everyone she encountered think she was the best thing since the Internet. From the lady at the dry cleaners who raved about what a wonderful woman my mother was, to the parents at her school who told me how lucky they were to have her as principal. To Alex, whom I'd talked to three times since we'd met and who told me Sarah was the best thing that ever happened to him.

If only all of them knew.

But no one knew.

And apparently, that was just the way Sarah Ford wanted it.

Today, though, I'd planned to set aside my fascination with my mother's re-created life and try to hear her valid explanation about why she just walked out of my life.

My body shook in anticipation. I hadn't planned to reveal myself in the middle of Starbucks, but I couldn't wait any longer.

When she'd dipped in the coffee shop this morning, instead of sitting in my car and watching her, I'd gotten out and followed her in. I don't think I'd ever been this nervous in my life. I stood behind her in line, knowing that any minute now she'd turn around, our eyes would meet, and she'd burst into apologetic tears. I had played the scenario out in my head countless times. And each time ended differently. Sometimes she'd take me in her arms and beg me for her forgiveness. Other times she'd say, "Oh well, you found me, now leave me alone."

My mother slowly turned in my direction and I grew tense as I wondered which scenario was about to unfold.

Her eyes met mine, and a smile formed on her lips. And a flutter passed through my heart.

"Hi," my mother said.

"H-hi," I replied, my voice just above a whisper.

I was just opening my mouth to say, "It's me, Brooke," when she said, "Do you mind if I reach around you and grab one of those boxes out of the basket?"

To say I was stunned would be an understatement. Her warm smile continued to greet me. I waited for a flash of recognition. When there was none, I stepped aside.

"Thanks," she said, reaching over me and picking up a

box of hot chocolate. "My little girl loves this pumpkin spice cocoa."

With that, she turned back around and placed her order.

THAT ENCOUNTER THIS MORNING had left me shaken, and unable to function most of the day. Sarah must have not gotten a good look at me. That's what I'd been telling myself all day. I know I was a grown woman now, but how could a mother not know her child? I was seven when she had left. Granted, I was a plump little child with a pudgy face, but I wasn't a baby. How could she not recognize me?

"So did you enjoy the book?"

Alex's voice snapped me out of my thoughts. He'd been all too excited when I called and asked him to meet me for dinner to discuss the book. Of course, my mind hadn't been on reading anything, but I had gone to Amazon to read some of the reviews just so we'd have something to talk about.

My mother had left me baffled, riding the fine line between anger and hurt. All day long I'd been asking myself the same question: Did she really not recognize me or was she playing some kind of game?

Now I didn't know when or how would be the best way to confront her.

What I did know, though, was that whatever my plan was going to be, it was going to involve the man sitting across from me.

"Yes, you were so right. That opening scene where the baby was burning, man that was heart-wrenching."

"I know, right!" His passion for reading made my heart smile. "Everyone should know about this book. The author hasn't released anything in a while, but hopefully, she'll come out of her literary hole and write something else."

"You really are into books, huh?"

His enthusiasm answered before he did. "I am. I always have been a voracious reader. My boys call me a nerd, but I just really love literature," he continued before taking a deep bite of his mushroom burger.

I don't know what prompted me to ask my next question.

"Can I ask, how old are you?"

He stopped chewing, swallowed, then with a smile said, "Does it matter?"

"Not really. You seem to be in your early twenties and it's just rare to meet someone like you who is so intelligent and well versed." I knew I was laying it on but I needed to butter him up if I was going to pump him for information.

"I'm working on my master's in American literature at Shaw University. Hence the bookstore."

"Wow, that's fascinating," I said, even though I had no idea what he planned to do with a literature degree.

We made more small talk, and I was amazed because Alex was really good conversation. But getting him to say much about his family was proving more challenging than I thought. I was able to tell how much he adored Sarah, whom he called Mom. (I cringed every time he said that.)

Alex was midsentence when he stopped talking, and his eyes darted away from the front door.

"Oh, no." A darkness spread over his eyes as he glared in the direction of the two women who had just walked in. "That's Kara. My ex."

My eyes shifted down to his hands, where he had all but crushed the water bottle he'd been holding.

I raised an eyebrow. "Are you okay?"

He didn't answer. Instead he just kept his eyes on the two women as they approached us.

"Well if it isn't psycho Alex," the shorter woman said.

"Jada, don't be like that," the other woman replied. Jada rolled her eyes.

It was obvious the two of them were related because they had the same smooth features and light brown hair.

"Sorry, Alex, you know how my sister is." The woman's voice was soothing.

"It's cool, Kara," he said with an eerie calmness. "When your baby daddy runs off and marries his other baby mama, it can make you bitter."

"You know what . . ." Jada said, taking a step toward Alex.

Kara stopped her just as Alex smirked and turned to me. "This is my friend, Mona."

Kara hesitated, like she just realized I was there. Then, with all the fakeness of Monopoly money, she said, "Oh, are you a relative?"

Before I could answer, he said, "Why? You don't think I could date someone like her?"

Jada cackled. "Boy, please. She's probably his customer, or a therapist."

I didn't know who these women were, but I really didn't like the way they were talking about Alex, so I spoke up. "Ummm, as a matter of fact, Alex and I are more than friends. We're dating." I covered his hands with mine.

Both women looked skeptical. Alex himself seemed shocked.

"And you would be?" I asked, a wide smile across my face.

"I-I'm Kara, his ex."

I playfully slapped Alex's hand. "You didn't tell me you had an ex."

"Wow," Kara said, obviously unintentionally because of the way she tried to immediately recover. "I mean, that's nice."

"So you're really here on a date with him?" Jada asked, like she still wasn't believing it.

I reached across the table and took his hands again. "Yes, Alex is the sweetest man I know."

Now his smile matched mine. I leaned in and stroked his cheek. I could tell the move made Kara sick.

"I hate to say this, but I'm glad things didn't work out between you two," I said.

"I'm calling bull," Jada said, defiantly crossing her arms. "Or she doesn't know you're—"

"Shut your face!" Alex screamed, jumping from his seat. "Or I'll shut it for you!"

The outburst caught us all by surprise because everyone— including the few customers around us—grew silent.

Kara's eyes were wide with fear, and the defiant cockiness that Jada bore just a few minutes ago was gone.

"C-come on, sis, let's go," Jada said, her tone now filled with fear.

Alex glared at them as they all but ran out of the restaurant. Within seconds, his brow relaxed and he exhaled. "So sorry about that," he said, looking at me. "Jada and I do not get along and she really pushes my buttons."

I sat still, not knowing what to say. That outburst was frightening. But his whole demeanor now was like he was a different person.

He set the crushed water bottle down on the table and continued: "Thank you so much for the whole dating thing, though. You have no idea how much that meant."

I managed to find my voice and said, "Uh . . . no problem. I just didn't like the condescending way they were treating you, especially that Jada chick."

"That's Kara's protective sister. She never did like me and she fought me every step of the way. Always said she thought Kara could do better than me."

He turned solemn.

"I really loved Kara, but . . ." His words trailed off, then he forced a smile. "Well, I owe you big-time," he continued. "The look on Kara's face was priceless because she thought I'd never be able to rebound after her. And I'm sure to see me with someone as beautiful as you had to mess with her. We should've kissed, that really would've blown her mind." He released a laugh that under any other circumstances I would've found quite disturbing.

Still, in that moment, I regretted the whole incident.

Before I could say anything else, his phone rang. He glanced at the screen. "Excuse me for a second, I need to grab this."

I nodded.

"What's up, Pops? . . . No, it's cool. I got you. I'm gonna need my money back. With interest . . . Yeah, it's not like she'll be surprised. You bring her a gift home every week . . . all right. I'll talk to you soon."

He pressed END on his conversation and turned his attention back to me. "Sorry about that. My dad wants me to pick up some white roses for my mom on the way home."

"White roses?" I asked.

"Yeah, he's real sappy like that. But I guess that's why she loves him like crazy. It's sickening actually. I used to think it was all for show, because when I was young, it was like she was trying too hard, you know?" The corner of his lip turned upward. "But I guess that's just how she is because regardless, I've never seen two people more in love."

"Well, aren't y'all the epitome of black love?" I had so many more questions, but I couldn't figure out how to bring them up without Alex questioning my prying.

"That's my parents," he said. "They're like the great American love story."

"Does that even exist?"

He shrugged. "For my parents it does. When I tell you my mom has given her all to my dad, to us. There's no doubt she loves this family." He laughed. "My friend Eric's father just cheated on his mom and the mom turned around and got her a side piece as well. I think if my dad ever stepped out on my mom—which he wouldn't—you'd have to commit her to a mental hospital. It would literally crush her."

Alex abruptly stopped talking and that darkness passed back over his eyes. "I know a thing or two about how that feels myself. That's why Kara and I aren't together. She cheated on me, claimed the dude was just a study partner, but I knew better. I bet Jada hooked them up." He said that like that piece of knowledge had just dawned on him.

"Anyway," he said, shaking his head like he was shaking off a bad memory, "I guess everyone isn't meant to have the perfect love story."

His flip-flopping emotions made me uneasy and I decided it was time to make my exit.

"Well, I'd better get going," I said, standing.

He stood with me. "Can we get together again? I really enjoy talking to you, Mona."

My first instinct was to tell him, "Naw, I'm good," but I had a feeling I would need Alex—at least until I figured this thing out with my mother. So I simply said, "Sounds like a plan. I'll be in touch."

CHAPTER 18

No wonder my boss had been so willing to let me work out of the Atlanta office. The amount of backlogged projects was ridiculous. I'd been knee-deep in files all day. In fact, I hadn't been able to do anything other than focus on work. A light tapping on my office door snapped me out of my work-induced haze.

"Hi, Brooke," the publicity assistant, Veronica, said. She'd been the one to greet me when I arrived. The poor girl—who couldn't be any more than twenty-two—was so happy to see me. She'd been holding down the office since the abrupt resignation of the lead publicist.

"Yes, Veronica?" I immediately took in her cute pastel peasant dress and Kate Spade flowered shoes. She may have not had the public relations down yet, but she definitely had the style.

Veronica shifted from one pump to the other, then flashed a nervous smile. "Can I just say how happy we are to have you in this office. It has been so chaotic since Miss Angela left. And well, we really need you."

"Thank you. I'm happy to be here. I will start doing interviews on Friday, so you should have a permanent publicist soon. In the meantime"—I pointed to all the files on my desk—"I'm knocking out as much as I can."

"Great. Here's another one. This notice that just came in. They wanted our firm to apply for a PR contract with the city of Atlanta. But we really don't do that, do we? We are strictly celebrity clientele, right?"

I was just about to say yes when it dawned on me what she'd just said.

City of Atlanta.

"May I see that?" I asked.

She gladly handed me the notice and I began reading. "The City of Atlanta is looking for a Public Relations Firm to handle a new Forward Prosperity campaign," I read. My eyes glossed over the rest of the copy, but came to a stop at the last line.

Will report to Deputy Mayor Anthony Ford.

"Umm, I'll handle this," I muttered.

"So we do do that kind of stuff?" she asked.

I feigned a smile. "No, but I want to bring this to Charlene's attention because it's something that we may consider later."

"Oh, okay. Well, I'm going to get back to work." The light tap of her heels filled the room as she all but sprinted from my office.

I continued looking over the notice.

Will report *to Deputy Mayor Anthony Ford.*

I had no desire in securing the city contract, but this would be a perfect in to try to get to know more. I didn't know how much more I could get from Alex, so this was definitely a viable option. I would get to know my mother from all angles.

I browsed through the specifics and noticed that the job closed in two days. That meant I needed to get to work.

. . . . . .

It was kind of sad that I didn't really want this contract because the plan I had put together in these past three hours was amazing, if I must say so myself. I relied on a news report that I'd seen last night and was able to come up with a proposal that I was sure would get me in the door.

I leaned back in my office chair and massaged my eyes. I probably needed to go home and get some rest, but then I glanced to the right and saw the mounds of paperwork that I'd been neglecting. No, I wouldn't be going anywhere anytime soon.

My cell phone rang just as I reached for the folder in the stack.

"See, the devil doesn't want me to do any work," I mumbled. I frowned in confusion at the international number. But just as I was about to press IGNORE, I figured it might be Tammy, my college roommate. We had only spoken via Facebook since I moved into her place.

"Hello," I answered.

"Hello from down under!" Tammy exclaimed.

"Hey, girl," I replied, happy to hear from her. "How's Australia?"

"It's good. I'm playing a she-warrior so you know I'm loving it."

I laughed, mainly because that role was right up her tomboy alley.

"So, are things good with my place?"

"Yes, it's awesome, you have no idea what a lifesaver you've been."

"Girl, you're helping me, keeping the criminals away."

We chatted a bit more, catching up on everything, before she said, "Did my cousin give you an envelope?"

"Oh yeah," I said. I had forgotten all about the envelope her cousin had given me when I went to pick up the keys.

"Cool, can you open it, and fax the forms in there to me today?" she asked.

"Of course," I said, grabbing a pen so I could jot down her fax number. "I'll send this over to you right away. Just shoot me a message on Facebook that you got it."

"Thank you so much. I have to get back on set. So you take care, and enjoy my place. If you get freaky with someone, don't do it in my bed."

"Bye, girl." I laughed.

I went over to the bag that I had stuffed her envelope in. When I pulled it out, I noticed the stack of letters I had written to my mother.

I'd brought them with me—well, I don't know why I brought them. I think I was hoping we could sit down and read them together.

I fingered the ones that had been opened, then the many more that had yet to be.

I decided to open one of them.

Dear Mom,

I just came back from my first date. Daddy didn't want to let me go, but I'm sixteen. It was nice. I went to the movies with Zach Baxter. I really like

him, Mom. But he tried to kiss me, then I freaked.
Then, he told me if I loved him, I would let him have
sex with me. I'm so confused. How can I love him if
this is just our first date? I mean, I know him from
around school, and I like him from there. But how
do I know when I'm in love? Will I really lose him
if I don't have sex with him? He said if I don't do
it, another girl will. Probably Melanie Willis, with
her skanky self. I have so many questions. I wish you
were here to answer them.

Love, Brooke.

I put the stack of letters away. I couldn't do it. There were so many times when I needed my mother, and to find out that she'd been alive the whole time was heartbreaking all over again.

No, we would read those together so she could explain herself. I grabbed the information I needed, faxed the forms to Tammy, and then went back to work.

CHAPTER 19

I sat in the lobby of Atlanta City Hall, fidgeting with the hem of my shirt. I'd mapped out my presentation strategy and was hoping to finagle a meeting with Anthony Ford. What I was torn about was whether I would tell him about his wife's little secret, or just pick him for information that might prove useful. I'd been nervous all morning, though. What if he knew about me? What if he'd been the one to force her to abandon me?

I almost chickened out several times.

Almost.

The idea of this new life that my mother had created overrode any desire I had to leave.

"Hi. I'm sorry, what did you say your name was again?" the receptionist asked, hanging up her phone call.

"Meredith. Meredith Logan," I said with a smile. It was going to be hard to keep track of all these names I was using but I didn't want to use Mona, in case Alex and his father ever got to talking.

She pored over her appointment book. I'd called before I

came to make sure he was in the office. Now I just needed to convince her to let me see him.

"I am so sorry. I don't see you on his schedule."

I kept my smile. "Well, I don't actually have an appointment. But I'm friends with his wife, Sarah, and she arranged for a quick meeting so I could give him my proposal for the PR campaign." I never had been great at lying and I was hoping she didn't see right through me.

She frowned. "He didn't say anything to me about it."

I chuckled. "Sarah said he was probably going to forget. But you can let him know I'll just drop it off and be on my way."

"You can give it to me and I'll make sure he gets it."

I pulled the manila folder close to my chest. "Oh, no can do. This proposal is top secret." I smiled, trying to ease her apprehension.

She was hesitant, but said, "Hold on, please." She picked up the receiver. "Mr. Ford," she whispered, "I have a Miss Meredith Logan here to see you. Umm, she says she's a friend of your wife here to drop off a proposal . . ."

I wondered why she was whispering since I was standing right in front of her and could hear her with ease.

". . . I know but she's pretty insistent . . . Okay. I'll let her know." She hung the phone up and looked at me. "Mr. Ford will see you now."

I reached over her desk and squeezed her hand. "Thank you so much."

She smiled. I hated that I had to resort to lies, but I was in war mode now. So, whatever it took, I was willing to do.

"Hi." Anthony Ford stood and extended his hand. He greeted me like he was supposed to know me but didn't want me to know he'd forgotten.

I reached for his hand. Shook it. I could see why my mother would be more physically attracted to him than to my father. He was even better looking than I'd initially imagined.

"Thank you so much for agreeing to see me, Mr. Ford. As deputy mayor, I know you're extremely busy, so I truly appreciate it."

"My pleasure," he said. "Now please have a seat."

He motioned to the chair in front of his desk, then waited for me to sit.

"So, my wife sent you?"

I rolled my lips in and sighed. "Okay, I have to confess, I am not your wife's friend. I am so sorry, but they were trying to make me turn my proposal in to your underling, and I knew that I needed to deliver this to you in person, myself."

I expected him to get angry, but he paused, then a slow smile spread across his mouth. "I like that. Innovative."

Whew. I relaxed. "Well, can I just say I really admire the work that you have been doing? And I know that ultimately, it's the mayor's decision on who they hire for this project, but we all know that it's usually the man beside the man who is the real boss."

My flattery was having its intended effect. He chuckled. "You got that right."

"I've put together a comprehensive PR plan on why our agency would be the best to let not just Atlanta—but the world—know about this revolutionary undertaking." I slid the packet across the desk to him.

He leaned up, opened the packet, which I had spent the last two days preparing, then began reading.

I could tell he was pleased because he nodded as he read. "Very impressive," he mumbled.

I seized the moment. "One of your constituents was on the news last night in a very poignant interview about how the city is taking her home of fifty-six years through eminent domain," I continued. "If you'll look on page four, I've developed a win-win strategy that could make people like the woman in that interview, Mrs. Bertha Mayes, the face of Atlanta Cares, a new project that allows the city to advance while taking care of the people who make up the very fabric of our community."

He sat back in his chair. I had no doubt impressed him, because his grin was wide. "Wow," he said. "You are good."

"And if the city hires my agency, I can be great." I'd hoped that after I made my pitch we could talk so that I could get more insight into him.

"Well, as you know, I have to take the presentation to the city council, but you have definitely sold me."

"Thank you so much." My mind raced for a transition to his personal life before he concluded the meeting. I saw the perfect in with the picture sitting on the corner of his desk.

"Oh my goodness. She is adorable," I said, pointing to the photo. "May I?"

He nodded, pride blanketing his face.

"That's my baby, Sunny," he said as I picked the picture up to study it. "She's six and the light of our lives."

"Your only child?" I asked. Maybe my mother had told him about me. Maybe he knew she had another child that, for whatever reason, she'd had to walk away from.

"I have an older son." He pointed to another photo in the corner of his office. It was Alex at his college graduation.

I set the picture back down on his desk. "When I eventually settle down, I think I want three kids," I said.

He laughed. "Two was more than enough for me. I was

always worried that my wife would want another child. Alex is her stepson. But once we had Sunny, she seemed content. And our family was complete."

His words had nearly knocked me off balance. I wanted to stay, pry more, have him say something that would help me make sense. But as the lump in my throat built, I took that as my cue for an early exit. "Well, thank you again, Mr. Ford. And I hope to hear from you soon."

I stood and felt his eyes roaming over my body, making me momentarily uncomfortable. He caught himself and said, "Oh, you definitely will."

I made my way back to my car. Outside of that last-minute ogling, Anthony Ford seemed like a really nice guy. Was that why my mother was content with never coming back? She'd found a nice man, a replacement family, and was living the perfect life?

Once I made it back to my car, I leaned against the headrest and tried to settle my pounding heart. I was getting bits and pieces of information from Alex and Anthony. I needed the whole story and it was evident the only place I'd get that from was my mother.

CHAPTER 20

When Charlene said working in the Atlanta office was going to be a lot more work, she wasn't kidding. This had turned into way more work than I wanted to do. But I knew if I wanted to stay here in Atlanta, I would have to make it work. And I couldn't do things like I'd been doing this morning—spending hours on the High Point Elementary School website, reading accolades about their "esteemed" principal.

I looked up from my desk to see Veronica, standing in my doorway.

"Hey, Veronica," I said, motioning for her to come in.

"I can't say this enough. I'm so glad you're here." She thrust a folder in my direction. "Especially now."

"What's going on?" I asked, taking the folder.

"Our client, Hype, just got caught up in a scandal, selling plagiarized SAT and ACT tests."

"What? Isn't Hype a gangsta rapper?"

"Yep."

"Wow," I said, perusing the papers. He rapped about killing cops and was hustling SAT tests? "Really?"

"You know, with the big cheating scandal Atlanta had with their school district a few years ago, the prosecutors are out for blood. Miss Charlene said to have you take the lead on this. Or you could take on the other one." She handed me another folder.

I groaned. This was the last thing I had time to be doing, dealing with high-profile cases.

"What's the other one?" I asked.

"The R-and-B singer Nina J. We've been representing her for about six months. She's getting bad press because she threw boiling water on her cheating husband."

I let out a heavy sigh. The expression on Veronica's face said she was hoping I would say that I would take on both cases.

"Okay, I'll take Nina J. You can handle Hype," I told her.

She looked horrified at the thought but I simply said, "Welcome to the big leagues."

"Guess I'd better get to work," she said, taking the first folder back from me.

"Me, too," I mumbled as she walked out of the office. I logged off the website, where I'd been reading about my mother winning principal of the year. I picked up the phone to dial Nina J.'s assistant.

"Hello, this is Brooke Hayes," I said when the woman picked up. "I'm the new publicist with First Impressions that will be handling Nina's situation."

"Thank God," the assistant cried. "This is her assistant, Amiya. Maybe you can get through to her because she is going off the deep end. She's on the radio as we speak."

"The radio?" I took a deep breath. "What station?"

"V-103." The assistant sounded completely exasperated.

I covered the mouthpiece and yelled for Veronica, who came running in.

"I need a radio!"

She looked confused, then said, "Who has a radio?"

"How do you listen to music?" I snapped. "V-103?"

"On my phone. I have the V-103 app."

"Can you turn it on?"

"One second." She ran back to her desk, grabbed her phone, and darted back into my office. She tapped the screen just in time to hear the deejay saying, "Hot water, though, Nina J.?"

Nina J. was not moved. "That's what's wrong with America! We're some pansies. We let people run all over us and we don't do anything about it."

"Are you listening?" the assistant cried through the phone. "She is out of control!"

I buried my head in my hands.

"What a man is not about to do is cause me pain without feeling some himself," Nina J. snapped to the deejay. "Nobody screws me over, because if it's one verse in the Bible I take to heart, it's an eye for an eye."

I groaned at her trying to twist the Bible to fit her narrative.

"I'm not sorry, and I'll do it again," Nina J. said, her voice filled with defiance.

"You have got to be kidding me," I mumbled.

The look on Veronica's face made me calm down. I was supposed to be setting an example for this aspiring publicist. I inhaled, and turned my attention back to the phone.

"Is she in the studio with him?"

"No, she's on the phone. This is a disaster. She won't listen to anyone," the assistant continued.

I took a deep breath. "Okay, when she gets off, please make sure she calls me and I'll handle it from there."

"Thank you," the assistant said, relief filling her voice. "Is this your number on my caller ID?"

"No, this is the office. I will text you my cell."

"He's lucky it's boiling water and not my twenty-two," Nina J. said just as I hung up the phone.

"Turn it off," I told Veronica, who did so, and slowly backed out of the room like she was grateful I was the one dealing with that drama.

I immediately began pulling together all the information I could find on Nina J. The task turned into a welcome distraction because it wasn't until my phone rang that I noticed it was well after 4 p.m.

I saw that it was April, FaceTiming me, so I hit ACCEPT.

"Hey, cuz, how's it going?"

"Crazy," I replied.

She sat up. "Did you finally see Aunt Sarah?"

"No, it's not that. Just a rough day at work." I leaned back and massaged my temples.

"So, wait, you're really working?"

"I know, right? And I just got thrust right in the middle of a public relations catastrophe," I said. "Anyway, how are things going there?"

"I'm bored silly. Ready to get these babies out."

"Well, you still have a minute."

"I should come down there and hang out with you for a while."

"As if Sam would ever let that happen."

Nostalgia passed over me as I thought about Trent. I hoped to have a husband care about me like Sam did April.

April brushed a curl out of her face and leaned into the camera. "So, don't play. You know I need a daily report until you figure out what you're going to do."

I stood and walked around my desk to close my office door.

"She saw me," I said, sliding back into my chair.

April's mouth dropped open in shock. "Get the freak out of here! And you're just now telling me? When? Where? What happened?" She pummeled me with questions.

I inhaled, exhaled, then told her all about seeing Sarah in Starbucks. "It's one thing when I thought she may have had amnesia, and may have literally forgotten about me," I continued, "but this woman hasn't given me a second thought. She looked me dead in the face and there was not a hint of recognition."

"Awww, I am so sorry, Brooke."

The memory hurt all over again. "I tried to tell myself that she was just a hell of an actor and knew who I was but my gut tells me she didn't. She didn't know her own child," I said, fighting back tears. "Then I went to see her husband, Anthony, yesterday."

"What?" April exclaimed. "Why?"

I shrugged. "I don't know. I'm just trying to make sense of this. Understand what it is about them that made her walk away from us."

"Ask her, Brooke. Just go ask her."

I wiped away the lone tear that had found its way down my cheek. "That's what I came here for. I was so excited, and now, just seeing everything . . . this life she's created . . ."

I could tell April felt helpless. "I hate this, Brooke." She paused. "Trent does, too. He called me and he's devastated about everything and thinks you're taking all of this too far.

Now, listening to you, I think he may be right. I don't know if this whole thing is a good idea, especially this following her around. That's slow torture. I think you need to go confront her, then come on back."

"I think you need to stop thinking," I replied, irritation replacing my impending sadness.

She pointed a finger at me like she was jabbing the screen.

"I understand this is a difficult time for you, so I'm going to let you make it. But you have one more time to snap at me . . ."

I sighed. "I'm sorry."

The sympathy returned to her face.

"I'm just saying, you don't sound like yourself and we all are really worried. You're getting all cozy with her stepson, who, I know you don't want to admit, is really feeling you, based on what you told me last time we talked. And now you're meeting up with her husband?"

"It's not like that. I just wanted to find out more about their family."

"How did you even hook up with him?"

"We didn't hook up."

I told her about the PR contract and how I finagled a meeting.

"So what about Alex?"

"What about him? I've gotten all the information I'm going to get from him."

"Then why are you still fooling with him."

"Look, it's lonely here. Alex is good company. That's it."

April shook her head, her face cloaked with worry. "You know how I feel about playing with people. I was just telling Symone that today. She got her revenge on Paul and that chick he was messing with, but now she needs to move on because playing with people's emotions can have you end up hurt."

"Well, I'm not Symone," I replied. "And it was just one meeting. But you don't have to worry because I am going to confront Sarah sooner rather than later."

"So what is your game plan exactly?" she said.

"I'm going to go talk to her. Soon. I just, I swear, I don't know if I can take her rejecting me again. I don't know what I will do if she does . . ."

"Brooke, just be careful. Too many people could end up hurt, not just your mother."

"Thanks for the warning," I said. "Now I really gotta go. I'll call you later." I pushed END before she was able to lecture me anymore.

CHAPTER 21

Atlanta had gotten lonely. Work had been taking up a lot of my time and my mother consumed what was left. The only socializing I got was my time with Alex, which I had come to enjoy, though not in any kind of sexual way. He just was good company. Though he was nearly ten years younger than me, in another lifetime I could've seen us being real friends.

"So, I know a lot of people make jokes about my literature degree, but I'm hoping to go back into the school system and be a teacher and ignite a love of reading in young people. In the technology age, that seems to be one of the main things we're losing."

I leaned back and smiled. Whenever Alex talked about literature, he had a light dancing in his eyes. That darkness I had seen the other day with his ex was nowhere to be found. Maybe he was right. Maybe it was only brought on because of his contentious relationship with Jada.

"You make me want to read more," I admitted. That wasn't

a line. He really did and once I got my mind back right, I vowed to get back into reading.

I had stopped by the bookstore after Alex called and begged me to come have coffee and pick up this new book. Since Nina J. and her drama had been stressing me out no end, I welcomed the diversion.

My compliment caused his cheeks to redden. "Wow, that means a lot. But that's what I'm hoping to be able to do with children."

He proceeded to tell me about some of the literacy programs he was working with, including one he had actually started at the YMCA with Kara.

"What happened with you and Kara?" I asked, cutting him off.

He stopped, seemingly taken aback by my question. "Ah . . . it just didn't work out."

"I know you said you thought she cheated, but do you know that for sure? I saw it in her eyes. She seems to really care about you."

He shook his head. "Nah, she doesn't."

"Please. I saw the expression on her face when I told her we were dating. That was like a dagger through her heart."

His eyes widened. "You think so?"

I nodded. "I know so. I know women and that woman loves you. I mean, you can tell me, is it you that cheated?" I flashed a sly smile.

His body stiffened and he was obviously offended by my question as he slammed his hand down on the table. "I am not a cheater. I despise cheaters."

"Whoa," I said, raising my hands in defense. "Sorry. I wasn't trying to imply that you were."

He relaxed, then shook his head like he was trying to shake away any residual anger at Kara. "No, I'm sorry. It's just that I . . . I don't know. Kara was my first love. And I got really upset because of that relationship with her study partner. Then things got a little rough between us and she bailed. I tried to get her to come back to me, and well . . ." He sat up. "You know what? I don't want to talk about Kara."

His words had such a finality that I decided to leave it alone.

"Well, thanks for the book. Do I need to pay for this?"

"Did I make you mad?" he asked, a worried expression across his face.

"No. I just need to get back to work." I'd told him that I worked at a PR agency, but I let him believe I was just a receptionist.

"Oh. Well, no, I already paid for the book." An apologetic look swept his face. "I really am sorry."

"It's okay, Alex." I stood.

He stood as well. "But my mom is bringing me dinner. I was hoping you'd get to meet her."

I froze.

"What?" I muttered.

"My mom should be here any minute now. I've told her all about you. I'd love for you guys to meet."

It took everything in my power not to freak out. I wasn't ready to face my mother! If she didn't recognize me again, I didn't know how I would react.

"That's nice, but I really have to go," I said.

I was about to do a Usain Bolt out of the door when Alex said, "Well, at least you'll get to meet her before you go." He looked over my shoulder. "Hey, Mom."

I remained frozen in place. Fear paralyzed me and kept me from turning around. I would make a scene if I ran.

Knowing I couldn't avoid the inevitable, I took a deep breath and turned around to face my mother. I had never been so nervous. I don't know why, maybe because deep down inside I was hoping that the coffee shop was a fluke and my mother would take one look at me and know. Or that she'd been thinking about me since she'd seen me in the coffee shop and she'd finally put two and two together. But judging from the huge grin on her face, I was being delusional.

"Well, I'm so glad to finally meet you," she said, reaching out to shake my hand. "Alex has been raving about this new friend of his and I was beginning to think she was a figment of his imagination."

"Mom, can you not embarrass me, please?"

"You're pretty." For the first time, I noticed the little girl standing next to her. Her long black ponytails hung past her shoulders. Her rosy cheeks and her unusually long eyelashes made her look like she belonged on the cover of an *American Doll* magazine. She was even prettier than her picture.

My sister.

"She is pretty, isn't she," my mother said, snapping me out of my trance.

I struggled to recover. From both the shock of coming face-to-face with my mother again and the fact that she still didn't recognize me.

"Th-thank you," I managed to say. I felt the anger bubbling inside me.

She studied me for a moment. "Have we met, though?"

"Mom, this is Mona," Alex said, thankfully taking her attention off me. "Mona, this is my mother, Sarah, and my sister, Sunny."

He took his food, which she had in a purple portable cooler. "Thanks so much for bringing me dinner." He turned to me. "Mom is an excellent cook."

"So I've been told." She chuckled. "Mona, you'll have to come over for dinner sometime. I'd really like to get to know more about you."

I had to squeeze my purse strap to settle my trembling hands. My mother was standing in my face. Inviting me to dinner. And she didn't recognize me. How could you not recognize the child you gave birth to? The thought made me want to throw up.

The moment she took one look at me, shouldn't she have known? The pain in my heart from the fact that she didn't know was unbearable.

"So Alex tells me you're not from around here," she said.

My first instinct was to lie. Lie, then run. But I sucked in as much air as my lungs would hold and said, "No, I'm not from around here. I'm from North Carolina."

She blinked. Then blinked again. And I just knew that was the moment.

Yet she relaxed, smiled, then said, "Well, what brings you to Atlanta?"

"Work." Then I don't know what made me say, "I'm a dancer."

Alex looked at me in shock. "What? You never told me that."

I shrugged, never taking my eyes off my mother. She had a

surprised expression as well and I could see the wheels churning in her head.

"Mommy is an awesome dancer," Sunny said. "She used to be a famous dancer."

"I don't call being a backup dancer for Mariah Carey a noted dancer," she said with a slight chuckle, though it was filled with uneasiness.

A backup dancer, I thought. *You left me to be a backup dancer?* "Wow," was all I could say. "With Mariah, huh?"

Either she was the greatest actor ever, or she had brushed off whatever seemed to be creeping into her mind. She smiled as she continued: "Yes, back in my heyday, I spent a little time on the road. I wanted to do something a little more classical, but I enjoyed getting to experience a little bit of my first love."

"She still teaches dancing on the side," Alex proudly said. "She has an amazing studio."

I glared at her. *The studio she didn't want my daddy to open.*

"That's nice," was all I managed to say. I turned to Alex. "Well, I really need to get going."

"You can't stay and have dinner with us?" Alex said. "It's my birthday and Mom brought me these homemade enchiladas since I had to work."

Again, that word. *Mom.* And again, I felt sick to my stomach.

"It's your birthday?" I managed to say. "Why didn't you tell me?"

He shrugged. "Mom always makes a big deal about it. But it would really mean a lot if you stayed and ate with us," he said.

As much as I would have loved to, if I stayed in my mother's presence for five more minutes I would have lost it.

"I'll have to take you out for a private celebration later," I said.

"Ooooooh," Sunny said, giggling.

"See you, later, Alex. And Sunny." I walked away without saying a word to my mother.

CHAPTER 22

$\mathcal{T}$he evening air outside the bookstore greeted me, engulfing me as if Mother Nature knew I needed comforting.

My chest heaved and I fought back angry tears as I leaned against the side of the bookstore trying to compose myself. I couldn't believe it. My mother hadn't recognized me *again*. I was being rejected *again*. And now I was on the verge of losing it. I just knew the "dancer" comment had gotten to her. And still nothing.

No. Whether I was ready or not, it was time. I couldn't live in this space between anger and hurt anymore. I needed to know why she left and what that meant for me now.

I paced up and down the sidewalk in front of the bookstore, waiting for her to come out. I didn't really want to do this in front of Sunny, but I couldn't go one more day.

The time was now.

"Mona?" she said when she spotted me. "You're still here?"

"Umm-hmmm," I muttered, shifting uncomfortably as I

glanced down at Sunny's hand, which was gripped tightly by my mother. "I was hoping we could talk."

When she hesitated, I thought she was about to protest. But she looked down at Sunny. "Sweetheart, go back inside to the kids' section and read a book. Mommy will be in to get you in a moment."

Sunny scurried back inside so we could talk.

"Yes, send your precious daughter back inside."

The coldness in my tone caused her to say, "Okay, did I do something to you, because I don't understand this vibe I'm getting from you."

I couldn't help but laugh. "This vibe. *This vibe.*"

I moved closer to her. I know I was frightening her because she tensed up. "Take a good look at me," I hissed.

She stared at me and shook her head as nothing registered. "Should I know you? You look vaguely familiar."

"Just, wow." I swallowed, silently demanding the tears not to surface. "Vaguely familiar? I look *vaguely familiar.*"

A perplexed expression crossed her face, and then, the moment that I'd been waiting for—recognition.

Her eyes widened in shock as her hand went to her mouth.

"Oh, my God. Brooke?" she gasped.

"Oh, so now you finally know who I am." I silently cursed because my tear ducts weren't cooperating and a wetness filled my face.

"Brookie, I can't believe it's really you." Her voice was just above a whisper.

"Don't call me that!" I snapped. "My name is Brooke."

She had the nerve to reach out to touch my face. "You're so beautiful. You've grown into such a—"

I slapped her hand away. "Don't you dare touch me."

My slap didn't faze her, because she stepped toward me, like she was still in shock.

"I—"

I couldn't even give her a chance to form her lie. I just said, "I thought you were dead!"

If she was hoping the tears welling up behind her eyelids were going to get any sympathy from me, she was definitely wrong.

"I'm so sorry," she whispered. "I . . . I, oh, my God, I can't believe you're here."

"You know, it's funny. I always heard that mothers had a bond with their daughters. But you would've never left if you had any kind of bond with me. You would've never left if you loved me. But hey, why worry about me? Just move to another city and make another me."

She was quiet as her hands shook.

"I can't believe this. I can't believe you're here."

"Yeah, I'm here because I just needed to see the woman who abandoned her own flesh and blood. I had to see her up close and personal. I needed to understand why. So imagine my surprise when I got here and saw your wonderful perfect life. Your woman-of-the-year, mother-of-the-year *Brady Bunch* life."

She looked like a child being scolded.

"I guess you've really fooled all of these people," I continued. "They don't know the real you."

"I'm a different woman now." Her voice was soft, almost desperate.

I glared at her. I had replayed this scenario countless times. Each time ended with me going off. Yet, when I opened my mouth, the only words that would come out were, "Why did you stop loving me?"

That's not the question I had hoped to ask. I had planned to curse her out.

Her eyes never left mine. "I never stopped loving you. Ever."

"Bull," I said. "Mothers who love their children don't leave."

She let her tears fall. "I left to save my life. I was miserable. I was dying. I don't expect you to understand, but I was no good to you the way I was."

"You're right," I said, stopping her before she could continue. "I don't understand. I'll never understand a mother who leaves her child."

Her shoulders rose, then fell, then she began fidgeting with the belt on her dress. "It was your father."

I jabbed a finger in her face. "You don't get to mention his name," I said, cutting her off before she got his name out. "He lived his life mourning you while you were up here living it up with some other man."

"Jacob is a good man," she said, ignoring my admonishment.

"*Was*," I corrected, disgusted that she didn't even know my father was dead.

Her hand went to her mouth. "My God. Jacob is dead?"

I refused to give her any details and simply said, "Don't act like you care."

Her shoulders sank. "I know you may not believe it, but I do."

I wasn't going to let her talk about my father, so I redirected my venom. "No, you can't believe I infiltrated your perfect little life; that's what it is, isn't it?" My words were pierced with twenty-five years' worth of hatred.

"I-I don't know what to say. It's so much more complicated than you could ever imagine."

I rolled my eyes and angrily wiped the tears from my face. "There is nothing for you to say. Complicated or not, you don't abandon your kid. End of story." I gritted my teeth. "You have no idea what you've done to me."

"Can we, oh my goodness . . ." She fanned herself. "What made you, I mean, why are you here?"

Those four little words packed an unimaginable punch. Sarah Ford had just found her daughter after twenty-five years and all she could say was, "Why are you here?"

Those four little words were like gasoline being poured onto a small brushfire.

I inhaled. Stood erect. I couldn't do this right now. I was too emotional and I wanted a clear head when I listened to her excuses.

"Don't worry, Mrs. Ford, your perfect pretend life is safe—for now."

I stomped toward my car, struggling not to burst into tears.

CHAPTER 23

I know that I'd walked away from her at the bookstore, but my mother had made no attempt in the past week to get in touch with me. And that caused the anger to overtake the hurt. Shoot, I might as well have filled out a change-of-address form for Pissed-Off Lane because that's where I now resided.

My mother had just let me walk away.

Just like she had done twenty-five years ago.

But I wasn't about to let her off that easy. That's why I was here, at High Point Elementary School, ready to share her secret, in front of her coworkers—if that's what it had to come to.

"Good afternoon!" The custodian flashed a crooked-tooth smile. "You need some help, lil' lady?"

His warm smile made me find my own. "Hi. Yes, which way to the front office?"

He pointed to the doors behind me. "You just passed it."

"Thank you." I nodded my appreciation and scurried toward the ornate double doors I'd just walked past.

"Hi, may I help you?" the woman at the front desk asked after I stepped into the front office.

"Yes, um, I'm here to see Mrs. Ford." I struggled to keep my voice from trembling.

"Oh, I'm sorry, sugar," the woman, who could have been anybody's grandmother, said. "Mrs. Ford is gone for the day."

I bit my bottom lip. Why in the world had I just assumed that she'd be here?

"Did you have an appointment? Or is there something I can help you with?" she asked.

I contemplated my next move. Finally, I said, "I'm considering putting my child in your school and was just looking around."

"Well, you're definitely in the right place." She stood and walked around the front desk. "As you can see, we're an award-winning school." She pointed to a wall filled with photos, certificates, and ribbons.

"Is that Mrs. Ford?" I asked, pointing to a picture of Sarah surrounded by a bunch of children.

"It is." The woman beamed with pride. "She is such a blessing to our children. I've never met a woman who had a heart for kids like she does." Adoration covered the woman's face to the point that I so wanted to burst her bubble and tell her the real deal about her beloved principal. "She treats each of these children as if they were her own," the woman continued.

"That's nice to hear," I finally managed to say.

"What grade is your child in?"

"Second," I quickly replied. The sight of my mother surrounded by a sea of adoring faces sent ripples of pain through my heart. I wondered if at any time that she was standing there, posing for this picture, she thought of her own daughter. Her oldest daughter.

"Boy or girl?" the woman asked.

"A little girl."

"Oh, our second graders are so precious. Your daughter will fit right in." The woman pointed to an empty spot on the wall. "We'll be placing a very prestigious award here next week," she said, her voice filled with pride.

"Really?"

"Yes, Mrs. Ford is nominated for a CNN Excellence Award. That's a tremendous honor. It's televised and everything. She's being recognized for her outstanding commitment to our young people. She was a product of the foster-care system and pulled herself up on her own, putting herself through school, and now she is giving back."

Either my mother had completely transformed or she was pulling some kind of number on these people.

"Well, would you like a tour of the campus?" the woman asked. "I'd be happy to show you around."

I feigned a smile. "No, I was actually hoping to see Mrs. Ford."

"Oh, I'm so sorry. She had to take her daughter to the doctor. She's out for the rest of the day."

I struggled to mask my frustration. "Okay, maybe some other time."

"Yes, you'll have to make plans to come back and meet our principal. You'll simply love her."

I did at one time, I thought.

"I'll keep that in mind," I said before hastily making my exit.

CNN?

Excellence Award?

"Not if I have anything to say about it," I mumbled as I pulled out my iPhone. "Siri, may I have directions to CNN?"

IT HAD TAKEN ME almost an hour to get a producer at CNN to come out and speak with me. I understood security, but you would have thought I was some kind of crazed terrorist the way they kept giving me the runaround. It wasn't until I called the CNN special events producer and convinced her that she needed to give me ten minutes of her time that I finally felt like I was getting somewhere.

"Mrs. Latimore?" a petite, white-haired woman said as she approached me.

"Yes." I stood and shook her hand. "Thank you for coming out to see me." On the drive over, I grew even angrier at the fact that not only was my mother not in hiding, but she was about to appear on a nationally televised program. You would think someone who abandoned her family would try to keep a low profile. But she was willing to appear on CNN? That meant she didn't give two damns about me.

"Well, you sounded pretty persistent," the producer said with a smile. "And truthfully, when you told me your information could save us a lot of embarrassment, I thought I needed to hear you out."

I nodded my appreciation. "I'm glad you did and I won't take up much of your time."

"So you said it was about one of our honorees for the CNN Excellence Award?"

"It is," I replied. "What is your criteria for the award?"

"A positive influence in the community, someone who goes above and beyond the call of duty."

"Sounds like it's a prestigious award."

"It is. Past recipients have included Maya Angelou and Oprah Winfrey."

"And my understanding is it also comes with a ten-thousand-dollar monetary award?"

"It does. But may I ask where you are going with this? You mentioned Sarah Ford on the phone." A veil of nervousness started to form across the woman's face.

"Do you all do background checks?" I continued.

"No." She eyed me skeptically.

"Hmmm, you probably should. In fact, if you did a background check on Sarah Ford, you'd be unpleasantly surprised."

"I don't understand. Mrs. Ford is a highly regarded principal in the Atlanta area and a noted community figure."

"Well, things aren't always what they seem," I replied.

Her eyes were wide as she said, "What does that mean?"

I shrugged. "You're the newsperson. You figure it out. Let's just say Sarah has a lot of secrets in her background, a secret past, a secret criminal record, secrets that could really affect the credibility of your award."

The producer's mouth opened in shock. "Secrets like what?" she asked.

"Let's just say she's not who she says she is. Her rags-to-riches story is the stuff novels are made of, and setting her up as an ambassador for your company will be something you will come to regret," I said matter-of-factly.

I could tell I had completely caught her off guard. Good. I hoped she went right back to her desk and started digging.

"Try the name Sarah Hayes or Sarah Watson," I added,

giving them her maiden name. And if I were you, I'd look in criminal databases, too." I was going to tear down Sarah Ford's perfect lie of a life brick by brick.

"Why are you telling us this? Do you know Sarah?"

"That's irrelevant." I slid my sunglasses back on. "I just thought you should know. And maybe rethink that honor. I have to get going."

She hurled more questions at me but I headed toward the door, satisfied that Sarah wouldn't be getting any CNN Excellence Award anytime soon.

CHAPTER 24

···

*M*y optimism had turned into full-blown pessimism
and all my dreams of a reality-show-worthy re-
union were out the window. My mother had no idea how
much her words outside that bookstore had hurt me. How
much her inability to embrace me cut to my core.

And I wasn't even sure she would care if she did know.

Why are you here?

Twenty-five years.

No tears of joy. No "Oh, how I've missed you."

Just, *Why are you here?*

Then any room I had left for pain, Trent had filled it up
when I called him to tell him about meeting my mother
and he acted disinterested, and ending up cutting our call
short.

The stress of these last few days had been like a boulder,
weighing on me to the point that I finally decided that a change
of scenery might help. So I was now sitting at a corner table
at the Bistro Cafe, letting my tomato basil soup simmer in my
bowl and talking to April on the phone. I'd just filled her in

on everything, and listened to her first get just as angry as me, then turn to trying to comfort me.

"Maybe she doesn't know how to get in touch with you." April said that like even she didn't believe it.

"All she has to do is ask her son. That just means she doesn't want to get in touch with me," I responded.

April sighed, sadness filling her voice. "So, are you going to go and try to talk to her later?"

I tested my soup, saw it was still too hot, then leaned back and replied, "Yeah, I still have so many questions, but I was just too emotional the other day." I think I had cried so many tears these past three days, I no longer had any tears to cry.

"She's probably somewhere freaking out, worried about what you're up to," April said.

"That's what makes this hurt so much," I continued. "I feel like all she is worried about is me messing up this fake life she's created. She's not the least bit worried about me, or establishing a relationship with me. It just pisses me off and I want her to know my pain."

"I know, sweetie. I'm so sorry," April said.

My eyes made their way to the front door of the restaurant, and the man who had just walked in.

"Oh, my, God," I muttered.

"What?" April asked.

"Sarah's husband, Anthony, just walked in."

"Oh, you should go over, tell him to meet you at the motel down the street, then put it on him. That would be the perfect payback for Sarah." April laughed.

I didn't.

The perfect payback.

"Uh, hellooo," April said once silence filled the phone. "Are you still there?"

"Yeah," I muttered as I watched Anthony. He was tapping away on his phone, oblivious to his surroundings. "The perfect payback," I muttered.

"What?" April paused, and when I didn't reply, her tone turned serious. "Ah, I was kidding," April said. "Brooke, do you hear me? It was a joke."

I nodded as my eyes followed him, taking in his lean build, wondering if I could bring myself to be with him.

"Brooke, are you still there?"

"Mmm-hmmm. Let me call you back."

"Brooke, what are you about to do?" April said, panicked. "Do not do anything with that woman's husband."

"Bye, April. I'll call you later."

Though my mother and her husband seemed happy, the way Anthony had looked at me in his office the other day, I was sure he had a wandering eye.

April was right. The perfect way to pay my mother back for all the hurt she'd caused me would be to seduce her husband.

That's not you.

I heard my cousin's voice as if she were in the same room with me.

I watched as Anthony got in line, placed his order and after paying, walked into the crowded lobby to look for a seat.

I shook away the devilish plan. Despite my issues with Trent, I was still engaged and hoping to soon be his wife. I couldn't be entertaining the idea of sleeping with another man. I could, however, take advantage of this opportunity that had all but dropped into my lap to feel him out for something more that I could use to damage my mother's little façade.

"Mr. Ford?" I said as he passed.

He stopped, and a smile spread across his face. "Meredith, right?" He walked over and shook my hand. "It's good to see you."

"Nice to see you, too," I replied, making sure my fingers lingered just long enough to cause his eyebrow to raise. I felt some kind of way about flirting with him, but I thought about my mother in that Barnes & Noble parking lot, then pushed those feelings aside. Besides, I was just flirting, trying to get information, nothing more.

"I passed your proposal on to the mayor, so hopefully you'll hear something soon," he said.

"Thank you." I'd planned to politely decline if we were actually awarded the contract, telling the city that we'd lost staff and couldn't take on new projects.

The waiter walked over with Anthony's order. "Are you order number 122?"

"Yeah. That's me," he said, holding up his ticket.

The waiter pointed to my table. "Is this where you're sitting?"

"Yes," I said, moving my bowl of soup. "You can set his plate here."

"Oh, no. I don't want to intrude," he said.

"You are no intrusion. Besides, you gotta take a break from work. And I could use the company."

That elicited another smile.

"Guess you're right," he said, sliding into the seat across from me. "My wife always says I'm such a workaholic and I was going to try and work through lunch, but I guess I need a break." His eyes roamed over me again, and this time I gave him more to see as I crossed my leg, just enough for the split in my plum wrap dress to open to reveal my toned thigh.

I ignored his gaze on my legs and said, "So, have you been married long?"

He caught himself, then lifted his eyes back up to meet mine. "Eleven years," he said as he spread his napkin across his lap.

I nodded, carefully weighing my next words as he bit into his club sandwich.

"I always heard that around year seven, you get the seven-year itch."

He stopped midchew, dabbed his mouth with his napkin, then said, "Yeah, marriage isn't easy."

"And not for everyone," I said, wiggling my ring finger at him. A quick pang shot through my heart as I thought of my engagement ring. I prayed that once this was all over, Trent would put it back on my finger.

"I can't believe a beautiful woman like you is single. Oh, excuse me," he quickly corrected. "I'm sorry. I didn't mean to be presumptuous. You're probably very much taken."

"No. You had it right the first time," I replied. "Very much single. I work a lot, too."

Like Alex, Anthony was easy to talk to. I could see why my mother would fall for him. What I had yet to figure out was, if they'd been married eleven years, what had my mom been doing for the fourteen years before that?

"You know, marketing was my first love in school," Anthony said. "I even majored in advertising and marketing. But then politics called my name."

"Oh, I have no doubt you'll go far in the political arena. I can see you one day being mayor, governor, senator, or better yet, you'll skip all that and go straight to president."

He laughed. "Nah. I wasn't exactly a model kid in college. That might keep me from being a president, but governor would be nice."

I put my hand on top of his. "I don't know you well, but if anybody can do it, I have a feeling you can."

He looked down at my hand as if I had sent an electric jolt through his body.

"You know, your work alone speaks for itself," he said. "You had the best proposal, period."

I wanted to bury my head in shame. I removed my hand. "I'm sorry. I wasn't meaning to be forward."

"I'm just teasing. Actually, I'm very flattered." Lust filled his eyes and made me question what I was doing, flirting for information. First the son, then the father?

There had to be a better way.

This was so out of character for me. I'd never in all my years flirted with a married man. I'd treasured the sanctity of marriage, and even though I was conflicted over the whole institution, I would have never thought I would lower myself to this for any reason.

My mother had turned me into someone I didn't know.

"Well, I need to get going," I replied. I'd barely touched my soup. But there was only so much rejection a woman could take. "I'll leave you to your lunch. You have a good day, okay." I stood and started gathering my things. I couldn't believe I'd stooped so low.

"No, wait," he said, gently grabbing my arm to stop me. I turned and the lustful look in his eyes wiped away my reservations. "I would love to see you again."

My heart sped up. The way he stroked my wrist, there was no doubt what he wanted.

I took a deep breath.

No, no, no.

"Yes," I said. "I'd like that."

He handed me his phone. "Type your number in," he commanded.

I pushed aside April's nagging voice and let the devil lead my fingertips.

CHAPTER 25

It had taken less than forty-eight hours for Anthony Ford to call my phone. And since my mother hadn't bothered to call my phone, seeing her husband's phone number pop up on my screen brought me a perverse joy.

I smiled as I answered. "Hello."

"Hi, is this Meredith?"

"It is."

"It's Anthony Ford."

I leaned back in my office chair and crossed my legs. I'd thought long and hard about this. Yes, I was flirting, and even contemplating doing something with him. But as long as I never crossed the line between thinking about doing and doing, I would be fine. And I would bear no guilt when it was time to fix things with Trent.

"Hello, Anthony. How are you doing today?"

"I'm doing well. Better now that I'm talking to you. How are you?" His voice was heavy with seduction.

The funny part is that, while he was handsome, I had no real physical attraction to him. I think it might have been the age difference. But the fact that my mother loved him so made me overlook that small issue.

"I'm well," I replied.

"Thanks for the conversation the other day. It was nice to just decompress and kinda forget about work for a minute," he said.

"Well, it was my pleasure."

He hesitated, then said, "So, look, are you busy tonight?"

That caused me to sit up.

He didn't waste any time.

"I ask because I'm going to a reception this evening and the mayor will be there and it would be nice if he could meet you since they plan to make a decision on the PR contract next week."

I grimaced and shifted in my chair. I didn't want to put my firm out there like that, so I had no desire to really meet the mayor.

"Oh, that sounds nice, but I have a full day."

"Oh. Well, if you change your mind, the reception is at seven. It should end about nine. I'll text you the address just in case you change your mind."

"Okay," I said.

AT 8:45, I DIALED Anthony's number.

"Hey, you," I said when he picked up. "I had all kinds of issues at work but if I'm not too late, I'd love to swing by the reception."

I could hear the disappointment in his voice. "Bummer. Things have just about wrapped up."

"Awww, are you still at the hotel?" I asked.

"I am. But most people have headed out. I was just going to go to the bar and have a drink while I finished up some paperwork."

"A drink sounds perfect," I said. "I'll be there in fifteen minutes." Maybe if I got a little liquor in his system, he would freely share information.

"I'll be here."

Twenty minutes later, I walked into the hotel bar area and immediately spotted Anthony sitting at a table in the back, looking through a stack of papers.

"Hey," he said, greeting me as I approached his table. He stood and kissed me on the cheek. "Ummm, you smell good."

"Jimmy Choo's Illicit," I said, flashing a flirtatious grin.

"Look at you being a naughty girl."

"Who, me?" I could tell he was enjoying my flirting. I wondered if my mother still flirted with him. I shook away that thought. Why was she always invading my headspace?

We talked a little about the event and when he brought up a project he was working on for a new community youth center, I saw my opening to get personal, especially since he was on his third drink.

"So, you mentioned the two kids. Are you planning to have any more?"

He hesitated, as if he was unsure how much to share. Finally, he said, "After my first wife died, I never expected to have any more children. But then, I remarried and my wife was in her midforties and desperately wanted a child before it was too late."

It was obvious it made him uncomfortable to talk about his wife. Still I said, "You don't see many women these days that hit their forties with no children."

"I know. She said God just hadn't blessed her and it was like she was obsessed with getting pregnant. Even though she was an amazing mother to my son, I think she felt incomplete at not being able to give birth to a child of her own."

I smiled because it was the only thing I could do to keep from crying.

He rubbed his temples like the drinks were getting to him. "I'd better slow down." He pushed his glass away. "But enough about me. Tell me a little about yourself. Where are you from? How long have you been here?" He loosened his tie to get comfortable.

"Well, what you see is what you get. I'm new to the Atlanta area." I decided against giving him any real information in case he decided to look me up. "In addition to PR, I'm working on my first novel."

"Nice. My son is heavily into books. In fact he's getting his master's in American literature. He's one of those career students."

I laughed.

Anthony and I sat and talked for another hour. I told him more lies about me. I felt like I was swimming in a cesspool of lies. He didn't bring up his wife anymore and I didn't ask.

But by the end of the night, I was sure about one thing: I couldn't let my mother get away with her happy re-created life. I wasn't ready to sleep with her husband—mainly be-cause of Trent—but I wouldn't leave Atlanta until I found some way to make her pay for the sins of the past.

CHAPTER 26

When I was growing up, my father had worked hard to make sure that I was loved. Though I had a huge hole in my heart from missing my mother, I had thrived because of his love. If I ever had kids—no, *when* I had kids—that's what I planned to emulate.

I'd been sitting in my living room all morning, trying to convince myself that I'd been loved enough. That I didn't need my mother.

But no matter how I tried to convince myself, my heart wouldn't buy it. It was probably because I was sitting here, reading more of the letters, reminding myself of just how much I'd missed her growing up.

I imagined what she was doing when I wrote this letter about losing my virginity at seventeen, to Marcus Berry, who then didn't have two words to say to me the next day. I'd written my mother three letters that week, heartbroken and devastated. And while I was writing, she was probably in New York, gyrating onstage to Mariah's "Always Be My Baby."

The thought made me take the stack of letters, stomp over to the kitchen trash, and dump all of them in.

I was standing over the trash, staring at my childhood, when the doorbell rang. I pulled myself together and walked back to the front.

"Who is it?"

"It's the police!"

My eyebrows scrunched together as I peered out the peep-hole. I broke out in a huge grin at the sight of my cousin.

I swung open the door. "April, what in the world?"

A gigantic grin spread across her face. "What's up, cuz?" She was standing there looking like a pregnant pencil.

"I can't believe you're here," was all I could reply.

"And I'm not alone," she said.

Symone peeked her head from around the corner where she had been standing. "Surprise."

"What are you guys doing here?" I said, hugging both of them. It wasn't until I felt the warmth of their bodies that I realized how much I had missed them. Well, April, anyway.

Symone spoke first. "Your cousin was gung ho on coming down here to check on you and of course I couldn't let her roll solo. We can't let her give birth to a baby on the side of the road with some farmer that stopped to help."

"Ha. Ha. Ha," April said. "But I got to go pee." She pushed past me and into the condo.

Symone followed her in, looking around the spacious condo. "This is nice. You just creating a whole new life and living it up down here, huh?"

"It was all fully furnished, so it's not my stuff. It's one of my friends from college's place. I didn't have to do anything but move in."

She leaned over and picked up a three-thousand-dollar vase. "Hmm, Monet. Your friend has some good taste."

"Yeah, she does," I said, taking the vase out of Symone's hand. "And I don't have any money to replace anything." I set it back down. "I cannot believe you guys are here," I repeated.

"Girl, April has been losing her mind," Symone said, plopping down on the love seat.

April came wobbling out of the bathroom. "Whew," she said, letting out a loud breath. "I thought I was gonna burst."

"You look like you are about to pop. I can't believe Sam let you come," I said.

"Well, actually he thinks I'm at the doctor." She giggled as she slid onto the sofa, then struggled to get her feet up on it.

Symone shook her head. "Girl, she's lying to the man to get away from him because he's suffocating her. Y'all just take these good men for granted."

April waved her comment off. "Whatever. I'll call him later and tell him that I had to come down here for an emergency."

"Now you're going to have Sam mad at me," I replied.

"Do you have some wine?" Symone asked, heading into the kitchen without waiting on a reply.

"There is some Stella Rosa in the refrigerator."

"Good. Just what I need," she called out.

I sat down on the other end of the sofa. "So, for real. What are you doing here?" I asked.

April's demeanor turned serious, as worry covered her face. "For real, I came to check on your behind and all your drama. And I could tell you were thinking nasty thoughts with your stepdaddy, so I came down to talk some sense into you."

"Would you not say 'stepdaddy?'" I said.

"That's what he is. Anyway, once I told Symone I was coming she insisted on driving me."

"Well, don't worry about me," I said. "I told you. I've got this all under control."

"I can't tell." She huffed and gave me one of those concerned little sister looks. "I'm not only worried about what's going on here. I'm also concerned about you and Trent. He is miserable."

"Bitter is more like it."

I looked up to see Symone leaning against the doorway with a glass of wine in her hand.

They exchanged glances. "Symone said Trent was at church and she thought he was actually crying during altar call," April said.

"Trent doesn't cry," I replied. "And it doesn't matter anyway. We're over." The fact that our conversations had been few and far between had me being overly pessimistic.

"So, you're done with him," Symone said. "Like for real?"

I shrugged. "Yeah, I guess so. Trent gave me an ultimatum and you know I don't do ultimatums. And then, we've just grown further apart with me being here." Of course, my heart didn't want to believe that it was over, but my head told me it was—at least until I came home. As long as I was in Atlanta dealing with my mom, Trent and I didn't stand a chance.

Symone was silent as she sat down. "I cannot believe you're going to let him get away," she finally muttered.

"Maybe it just isn't our time," I said. "Who knows what the future holds."

"So, you're just going to sit him on the shelf until you can get to him?" Symone asked.

"I didn't say all of that. It's just the whole way he reacted about all of this. It had me rethinking things anyway. Everything happens for a reason."

Symone pursed her lips like she was deep in thought, but April shook her head. "I refuse to believe that," she said. "You two were meant for each other. Now how are y'all gonna have these pretty little babies?"

"Girl, I told you I wasn't about to have any kids anytime soon. That in itself would have been another problem for Trent. So, like I said, it's all for the best."

Symone was unusually quiet. I was glad since I wanted to change the subject.

"Any more drama in your life?" I asked her.

She shook her head as she sipped her wine, relaxing as she leaned back. "No, girl. I'm drama-free ever since I cut Paul loose. He moved in with Skeezer-Ho and then she got back with her husband and so she put him out. That's what he gets. Now I'm just trying to live a drama-free life," she said.

Drama-free. That's what I wanted. The problem was, I didn't know when I would get it.

CHAPTER 27

*E*very time I thought I couldn't feel any more pain, my mother managed to make sure that I did. I was truly beginning to like the obsessed nutjob that Trent was painting me out to be. I felt like I was spiraling in a bottomless, hate-filled pit. And the only thing that would pull me out was revenge.

The funny thing is, the whole time April and Symone were here, I had pushed aside my thoughts of revenge and just had a good time hanging with my girls.

But the minutes they hit the road, heading back to Raleigh, I was back to my black hole. And I'd stayed there all week. I'd passed out at work, dehydrated I guess. So I'd been off for the past two days, and bored out of my mind.

Anthony had been out of town, but we'd spoken by phone a few times. I was beginning to feel like I'd drained all the information from him that I was going to get. Same thing with Alex. And so I'd kept my distance all week, which caused the loneliness to set in. And my longing for Trent to intensify.

Trent.

I'd been trying not to think about him. All of my calls and texts this week had gone unanswered.

This morning, he'd finally called. Instead of being happy to talk, we'd ended up arguing again. He'd told me since I "was only thinking about myself," he was going to do the same and had decided to reenlist. That broke my heart.

I shook off thoughts of Trent and refocused on the issue at hand—following my mother through the mall. Since I was feeling much better, I had wanted to get out of the house. And of course, I'd ended up in front of my mother's home.

She and Sunny had come out, and oblivious to my car parked across the street, hopped into her car and headed here to the mall.

I was like a zombie as I followed them through the complex, wondering where they were going in their matching hunter-green dresses. Watching them set my heart on fire. When they stepped into the portrait studio, it caused a full-blown inferno. We never took mother-daughter pictures.

That's because she didn't want to be your mother.

I pushed aside the voice that had been relentlessly taunting me since I set foot in Atlanta.

They walked up to the counter in the portrait studio and I dipped into Abercrombie & Fitch, which was right next door.

I browsed around, snapped at the saleswoman who asked if I needed help, and, after I felt like my mother and Sunny were in the back to take their pictures, walked back out.

Sure enough, Sarah and Sunny were in the front bay. A couple of people had stopped to watch the photo shoot.

"Aren't they adorable?" one woman said as I approached the window.

"I can't wait to do that," said another pregnant woman as she rubbed her stomach. Her husband pulled her closer.

"Soon," he said, massaging her belly.

Sunny made funny faces at the camera, which caused my mother to laugh.

If it hadn't been my mother and my sister, I too would have been enamored with their photo shoot. But right now all I felt was contempt at their picture-perfect life. As soon as the thought entered my head, I reminded myself about Anthony and how he was all too ready to hook up with me. My mother's life wasn't as perfect as she wanted everyone to believe.

The pregnant couple walked away. Another lady came and smiled and watched them take pictures.

Sunny looked like a child model as she struck a pose and lit up the room. She was obviously full of personality, and you could tell my mother and the photographer were simply captivated by her.

It made my heart hurt. For a number of reasons. Of course, that she'd taken my life. But at the contempt I felt for her. You weren't supposed to hate a child. And yet, I hated her.

After Sunny took a round of pictures, my mother scooted in next to her. She sat on the floor and Sunny sat next to her. The photographer took a few shots. My mother adjusted Sunny's hair and a tear slid down my face. I wiped it away and promised myself that she would get no more of my tears.

Just as I was about to turn to leave, her eyes locked with mine through the window. She furrowed her brow and lost her smile as she studied me for a minute. I wished that I could read her mind, just glimpse what she was thinking.

Sunny put her hand to my mother's face, trying to get her attention focused back on the photographer, and my mother smiled. As soon as the lightbulb flashed, she looked back out at me and I took that as my cue.

I walked into the studio.

"Since we're taking mother-daughter photos, can I join you?" I asked.

The photographer looked confused. Sunny was too busy adjusting her skirt to notice my mother as she jumped up.

"Can you give me a second?" she asked the photographer, who simply nodded.

"What are you doing, Brooke?"

"I'm just trying to get into the mother-daughter picture. Since you know, we never took one. Better late than never, huh?" My sarcasm was on full display.

Her shoulders dipped in exasperation. "What do you want me to say?"

"I don't know, anything. Something." I just knew I didn't want her acting like I was some kind of inconvenience.

"Is it a relationship you want?"

Just the way she said it was like a thousand knives through my heart. "You know what? I don't want a damn thing from you. I came to Atlanta thinking that I did. I came here hoping for something." My voice cracked. "But I guess I was just being delusional."

"I hate that you feel that way but you've got to let me explain." She sighed. "I want to talk to you. Just not here. Not in front of . . ." She looked back over her shoulder at Sunny, who was posing as she tried on a pair of sunglasses.

"Your daughter." I finished the sentence for her. "You know what? I'm good. You've said what you needed to say."

She wrung her hands in frustration. "I know I'm not handling this the right way, but I do want to talk to you."

"Mommy," Sunny called. "Come on."

"Let me finish up here," my mother said. "Can you wait?"

"No. Go see about your daughter," I said, cursing the tear that had found its way out.

She took my hand, and though I wanted to snatch it away, I relished her touch. "Please, Brooke, can you come by my school so we can talk? After school, please. I work at—"

"I know where you work," I said, cutting her off. "Fine. I'll be there. I need to hear this doozy of a lie in detail."

She didn't reply, instead just squeezed my hand and said, "I'll see you then." And then walked away.

CHAPTER 28

....

I needed to let Alex go. I already felt bad about using him, because he really was a nice guy. But it was just a matter of time before the truth about me came out.

That's why I'd agreed to let him come by when he called and said he wanted to bring me something. I hadn't figured out how I'd break our friendship off. I just knew that I would.

"Hey, come on in," I said, opening the door. Though we'd met up often, this was his first time at my place.

He leaned in, kissed my cheek, and made his way inside. "Hey, beautiful." He looked around. "Nice apartment."

"This is a friend's place. She's hardly here, so it worked out perfectly."

He smiled, then handed me a book. I should have known that was what he wanted to bring.

"Well, thanks for letting me swing by. I just wanted to bring you an advance copy of Daniel Black's new book."

"Thanks," I said, taking it.

Maybe one day I actually would get into reading.

"I was also hoping you could take a look at my essay for my contemporary lit class."

I sighed. Reading a college essay was nowhere on the list of things I wanted to do today. Still, I said, "Sure."

"Thanks. Do you have anything to drink?" he asked as he sat down, pulled some books out of his backpack, and opened them up like he was going to be here a while.

My doorbell rang just as I was about to head to the kitchen. I made a U-turn and went to open the door. My mouth fell open in shock when I glanced out the peephole.

I swung the door open. "What are you doing here?"

"Hello to you, too."

The sight of my ex-fiancé made my heart flutter. In an I-miss-you-and-what-the-hell-are-you-doing-popping-up kind of way. He wore jeans and Timberland boots and a purple pullover. Another time, another place, I would have been unable to contain my desire.

"I need to talk to you. Can I come in?" he asked.

"How did you know my address?"

"April gave it to me."

I made a mental note to curse my cousin out.

"Don't be mad at her," he continued. "She told me she came down and she is seriously worried about you." When I didn't move, he repeated, "Again, can we talk?"

I looked back over my shoulder. Alex was watching me with hawk eyes.

"Fine," I said, and stepped aside.

Alex immediately stood. Trent didn't bother to hide his shock as he stepped into the living room.

"Oh . . . you have company?" The hurt in his voice hurt my heart and I quickly stepped up to explain.

"Alex, this is Trent. Trent, Alex."

Alex gave a "what's up" nod.

Trent didn't bother to return his greeting. Instead he turned to me. "Are you tutoring?" he asked, motioning toward the textbooks Alex had strewn out on the coffee table.

"And you would be?" Alex asked, which of course, caused Trent to buck up.

"Her fiancé," he said, taking a step in Alex's face. "Who the hell are you?"

I immediately stepped in between them. "Trent is my *ex*-fiancé," I reminded him. "Alex, excuse us, please." I grabbed Trent's hand and all but dragged him out the front door.

"You have a lot of nerve," I said once we were outside. "What in the world are you doing here?"

His eyebrows scrunched together, his signature move when he was fighting back fury. "I came to Atlanta thinking maybe I could come talk some sense into my fiancée, but obviously, it looks like you've moved on."

I sighed. "Trent, this is not what it seems."

"Said every person who's ever been busted cheating," he snapped.

"Really? I am not cheating, Trent." I grabbed his arm and pulled him farther away from the door.

"So is that why you didn't want to marry me?" he asked. The pain in his voice sent a pang in my heart.

"Don't be ridiculous, Trent." I released a frustrated sigh. "That's Sarah's son."

"Your mother, Sarah?" he asked.

He paused. Looked back toward the door, then back at me.

"Yes." I folded my arms and looked behind me to make sure Alex hadn't opened the door. "Her stepson. She adopted him when he was thirteen."

"Oh." He looked confused. "So why didn't you introduce him as that?"

"Because he doesn't know who *I* am."

"What?"

"Look, I befriended him and I'm just trying to get some information." I hated telling Trent all the details, since he hadn't been supportive of this whole thing, but I didn't want him to think I was getting with another guy—despite the fact that we'd broken up.

Alex opened the door and stepped out.

"Everything okay?" he asked.

"Yes," I replied. "Just let me finish this, then I'll be right in."

Trent stared at me like he couldn't believe any of this. Alex hesitated, then took a protective step toward me.

"Really?" Trent said with a slight chuckle. "Yo, bruh. This doesn't have anything to do with you."

"I'm not your bruh," Alex replied. He was slowly balling and unballing his fists. "And I'm just making sure Mona's okay."

Trent cocked his head and gave me a look, then turned back to Alex. "Well, considering that she's my fiancée, you don't need to check me," Trent said.

Alex stepped closer, not the least bit intimidated, even though Trent had to have at least four inches and forty pounds on him.

"Dude, this ain't what you want," Trent said.

I put a hand on Alex's arm. "Really, Alex. I'm okay. Just go back inside. I'll be in in a minute."

"Yeah, *son*. You heard her. Go back inside." While Trent never had been one to back down, he wasn't the aggressive type, so this whole tough-guy persona was out of character for him.

"I got your 'son,'" Alex said.

Before I could say anything else, Alex charged Trent. It only took a second for Trent to break out his military training and put Alex in a headlock.

"Stop!" I screamed.

Alex flailed, trying to break free.

Trent squeezed, lifting Alex like he was a rag doll. "You want to try me, lil' boy?"

"Trent, let him go!" I screamed, pulling at his arm.

Trent's grip was strong but Alex wasn't giving in. He kicked and slapped at Trent. It didn't faze Trent.

"I'll let you go but you'd better calm down before you get hurt," Trent said, shaking him.

"Please, let him go," I cried.

Trent released his grip, pushing Alex up against the wall. I thought the rage in Alex's eyes was going to propel him to charge again. But he must have realized that he was no match because he stood, glaring, his cheeks puffed, his chest heaving.

"Alex, please. It's okay. Just go back inside," I pleaded, my hand on his chest.

He paused a second, but then turned and went back in.

"You'd better get your little brother in check," Trent hissed, jabbing a finger in my face.

"Would you stop saying that?" I whispered. "And what's with you and this Rambo act?

"I don't start fights, but I will end them." He paced the

walkway, trying to calm himself down. "And who the hell is Mona?"

I sighed, wondering how this day had escalated into this drama.

"I couldn't very well tell him my name," I said.

I could tell Trent was exasperated with me. He liked structure, and control, and having this situation be beyond his control was frustrating on a whole other level.

"But I still don't understand why you're here," I said. "You haven't returned my calls or texts and you just show up here? What's up with that?"

"I told you. I'm tired, Brooke. You need to shut this down and come home."

"Don't worry about me. I got this."

"So, it's like that?"

"Just go back to Raleigh and if I need you, I'll let you know."

He stood, staring at me. His tone was much calmer now. And bore an eeriness that frightened me. "So, it doesn't matter to you that our relationship is falling apart?"

"If our relationship couldn't survive this, we don't have much of a relationship."

He bit his lip as he shook his head. "If you send me away . . . if you don't put an end to it . . ."

"What, Trent?" I said. Now I was exasperated. "You'll leave for good? News flash, you're already planning to do that. You signed back up for the Navy, you're moving to Norfolk. You broke up with me. You moved on, so it shouldn't matter what I do. But you know what?" I was on a roll now. "It's probably best anyway. Because I'm not interested in a caveman for a husband." I don't know what made me say that. I didn't want to lose Trent for good. But I was livid.

A heavy silence momentarily hung between us. Finally, he said, "I hope you know what you're doing. With your mom and with us."

He turned and walked away without another word.

I took a deep breath, fought the urge to go after him, pushed the tears back, then headed back inside, hoping that Alex had calmed down.

"Everything okay?" Alex asked once I was back in the condo. While his lips were still pursed, his rage had been replaced with worry.

"Yes, I'm fine. My ex is just having a hard time with our breakup." I plopped down on the sofa. Trent had truly rattled me.

Alex looked at me with the strangest expression. "I can understand why. I wouldn't want to let you go, either."

He scooted closer to me on the sofa.

"I hate seeing you so upset."

I closed my eyes, inhaled, and replied, "I'll be okay."

I had just opened my eyes when I saw Alex leaning in, his puckered lips just inches from my face.

I held up a hand to stop him. "Whoa!"

His eyes shot open and he quickly moved away, flustered. "I know, I know. I'm sorry. I . . . I didn't . . . I know that I'm not your type."

The hurt in his eyes made me say, "It's not that. I'm just not looking for a relationship."

"So you're not mad?"

I shook my head. "No. I just want to make sure we're on

the same page." I cocked my head and punctuated my words. "We're just friends."

He nodded, then released a big smile. "Just friends."

I relaxed until he added, "Just friends for now."

Yep, it was time to let Alex go.

CHAPTER 29

My fight with Trent had messed me up. I'd tossed with anger, turned with regret, and awakened with a resolve. I didn't want to lose my man.

After doing something that I rarely do—fix breakfast—I'd sent Trent a text.

U still in town? Can u come over and talk?

I saw the three dots that let me know he was typing. I waited with anticipation until the message appeared.

Naw. Back in Raleigh. I'm good. Do u.

Do u?

The realization hit me like an eighteen-wheeler: I was really losing my fiancé. No, I couldn't let that happen. That's why by 1 p.m. I was on my way to Raleigh.

I was going to fix this with Trent. Plus, I needed to check

on my grandmother anyway. I also needed to get some more clothes and check on my place.

On the drive up I-85, I kept telling myself Trent had every right to be angry. I had all but abandoned him and had not taken his feelings into consideration. And for what? To establish a relationship with a woman who clearly didn't want one. As I neared Trent's exit, I dialed his number.

"Hello," he said. He had ignored my last three calls, so I was caught off guard when he picked up.

"Hey."

"What's up, Brooke?" His tone was dry and caused a lump to form in my throat. It hurt to hear the coldness in his tone.

"Nothing," I replied. "How are you?"

"I'm fine. Is there something you need?"

Wow. I pushed aside any retaliatory reactions and prepared the speech I'd practiced all the way back to Raleigh. I wanted to tell him he was right about me easily relocating to Norfolk. I wanted to promise that as soon as I finished up this business with my mother, we could focus on that. Ask him not to give up on me and be patient as I worked through this mess with my mother and completed my work in Atlanta. I wanted to beg him to give me just a little more time. Instead all I said was, "I was just wondering if I could come by so we can talk?"

"Naw. Maybe some other time. I'm kind of busy."

I could have sworn I heard giggling in the background. When I listened harder, I heard nothing and told myself it was just my imagination.

"But I really need to talk. I came home just to talk to you," I said, pushing down the sickening feeling in my stomach.

"Oh, kinda like I did with you yesterday?"

"I'm sorry about that. I feel awful about how that all went. We . . . we just need to talk."

"Like I said, I'm still busy."

I strained closer to the phone. I did hear giggling.

"Trent, what's going on? Do you have somebody there?" I asked.

He let out a cackle. "You don't get to ask me that. What we do isn't each other's business, remember? We're not together because it's for the best, remember? But I'm going to have to call you later."

And then he hung up before I could say another word. I immediately called him back and he sent me to voice mail on the first ring.

His exit loomed, telling me and the crazy girlfriend inside me to make a quick swerve and get off. I had never been one of those women who show up unannounced at their boyfriends' house, but the way he just talked sent a sickening feeling to my stomach.

I listened to the crazy voice and made a sharp right turn off the freeway.

I got to Trent's apartment in five minutes. I swung into a parking spot in front of his unit, jumped out, raced up the walkway, and banged on the door. He opened it like he knew I was coming.

"Are you serious?" he said. "Brooke, what are you doing?"

I peered over his shoulder, fidgeting at the thought of what I might find. "Can I come in?"

Trent paused, and I knew he was about to come up with some kind of excuse, but then he stepped to the side. I couldn't help it. I stomped in, went back to his bedroom, and then came back out.

"Really, Brooke?" he said, folding his arms and watching me search his house like I was the FBI. "What are you looking for? What do you think you're going to find?"

I realized that no one was there and I felt like a fool. "I-I . . . I'm sorry. I."

He stepped closer to me, an angry smirk across his face. "You thought you could put me on a shelf while you go on this quest for your mother. You thought you could just toss me and my feelings aside and come roll through here whenever you felt like it."

I sighed. "Look, Trent. I'm sorry. I just wanted . . . I thought you would be more understanding."

He wasn't moved by my words because he yelled, "We're supposed to get married and you threw us all away to go do what?"

"I needed answers." My voice was just above a whisper as I mumbled the words I'd muttered more than a hundred times.

"And do you have them?"

"No."

"Well, go back to Atlanta and get them. Go back to your brother-slash-boyfriend."

"I told you what I was trying to do with Alex."

"And I told you, you need help. I'm tired of this game, Brooke. I'm ready to get married, settle down. I'm ready to start a family. And I don't have time to wait for you to go on some wild goose chase that you don't even know where it will lead you."

Tears welled up in my eyes. And the compassionate, loving Trent I'd fallen in love with was still not moved. I had pushed him to his limit.

I tried to find my voice to tell him that I did want to still marry him, I did want to move to Norfolk and start a life with him. But I knew that the minute I uttered those words, he wouldn't want me to go back to Atlanta; yet my mission there wasn't yet complete.

"All I know is I'm not doing this back-and-forth with you," Trent continued. "So, you go back to Atlanta. Go back to your mother and then once you're finished doing whatever it is you're trying to do, we can talk. I may be around or I may not."

He walked back over to the door and my heart crushed as he opened it for me to leave.

"I-I admit I acted irrationally," I stammered, finally finding my voice.

"Are you done? Are you done with this thing with your mother?" he asked.

"No . . ." I slowly shook my head.

"Then call me when you are."

The look on his face told me he was done talking. I stepped through the door and when I turned to say something, he slammed it in my face. I felt so foolish. What was I doing here? And then, to think I'd come to try to catch him doing something wrong. I made my way back down to my car and had just reached for my passenger door when a little red BMW pulled in next to me. I paused to get out of the way so her door didn't hit mine and then stopped when I saw who was getting out of the car.

I stood as she reached into her backseat and grabbed her Louis Vuitton duffle bag.

She froze when she saw me.

"Wh-what are you doing here?" she said.

"Umm, no. I think I should ask you the same question," I said.

"I . . . I . . ."

My eyes went to the duffel bag.

"You know someone over here?" I asked.

Symone's eyes shifted away from me and my radar went into overdrive.

Y'all gon' get enough of letting these good men get away.

"Are you here to see Trent?" I asked when she didn't answer.

She paused, looked upstairs toward his apartment, then finally, with an unbridled cockiness, said, "I am. I've been here all night. I was gonna go home and get dressed but my meeting got pushed up so I turned around to come back here and get dressed."

I was speechless. Symone, one of my closest friends, was sleeping with my man? "What the hell is going on?" I asked.

She folded her arms, her stance turning defiant. "Look, don't get mad at me. You broke up with him. And he still wanted to make it work. Even when I told him you moved on and to give us a shot, he wanted one more chance with you. That's why he came to see you. Guess he needed to see for himself."

"Wow," I said, too angry to cry. "So that means that you swoop in to pick up the pieces?"

"Trent has been lonely since you bailed on him. And I, I mean I wasn't trying to, it just happened."

I stood, staring at Symone in disbelief. "*What* just happened?"

"Us." She rolled her eyes, like I was the one in the wrong. "I don't know why you're tripping. You moved on from him."

My eyes went to her bag again. I recalled the giggling and how Trent didn't want me to come over. Symone wasn't slick. She'd come back to let me know that she'd been here.

A part of me wanted to stomp back upstairs with her and get to the bottom of this. But I had had enough of the crazy-girlfriend role for today. Besides, this was the ultimate betrayal.

"If it makes you feel better, he wouldn't sleep with me until he was sure you didn't want him." She shrugged nonchalantly.

I wanted so bad to slap that smirk off her face, grab her by her twenty-four-inch Malaysian yaky, and drag her across the parking lot. But I'd embarrassed myself enough for one day. "I hope you guys are happy. I hope he was worth our friendship."

"Friendship?" She laughed. "It was never that deep."

"Wow," was all I could say.

She glanced up at Trent's apartment, then back at me. Her defiant stance softened. "Look, I really wasn't trying—"

I held up my hand to stop her lame excuse. "Save it. Do you. Just know, karma ain't no joke."

I jumped in my car and sped off before she could see just how heartbroken I really was.

CHAPTER 30

....

I never made it to my grandmother's. I just couldn't face her—or more questions. I'd gone home, grabbed some more clothes, and watered my ivies and was back on the road in thirty minutes.

I'd talked to April (telling her everything about Trent and Symone and telling her to go get Penelope from Trent) and done four business calls, including one two-hour call with Nina J.'s management team on my drive back to Atlanta. I just needed to keep busy. But now that I was ten minutes away from home, I had no one left to call and the tears that I had been fighting back finally surfaced.

I cried for my relationships—with my mother and with Trent. I cried because I'd wondered if everyone was right. This quest for revenge was costing me more than I ever imagined. And had I driven Trent into another woman's arms?

No. I shook that thought off. Trent was a grown man. His actions should never be a *reaction* to mine.

My phone rang and I saw Alex's number pop up on the screen. I answered only because I needed the distraction.

"Hey, Mona. I think I left my literature textbook over there," he said. "Can you check on your coffee table?"

"I'm not home, but I'll be there in about twenty minutes."

A beat hung in the air.

"What's wrong?" Of course, he could tell something was wrong. Alex was intuitive.

Still, I said, "Nothing."

"Come on, Mona. I can tell something is wrong. Stop shutting me out. Let me be there for you. As a friend." The concern in his voice warmed my heart.

"Nothing's wrong," I repeated.

"How far are you from home?"

"About ten minutes."

"I'm going to meet you at your house." It was a statement, not a question.

"Alex, you don't have to—"

"I'll be there in thirty minutes. I'm bringing Ben & Jerry's. You know we have to support them because they're down with the cause."

For the first time since I'd found out my fiancé was screwing my friend, I smiled. Maybe Alex's company would be just the distraction I needed.

"Okay. See you soon."

THIRTY MINUTES LATER WE were sitting on my sofa, a bowl of Chunky Monkey in front of us.

"Okay, tell me what he did and who I need to go beat up."

I chuckled, then just decided to come clean. "I just found out my ex and one of my friends slept together."

Without missing a beat, he added, "Then obviously, she wasn't your friend."

"You're right about that. The bad part is I've known that all along." I dipped the spoon into the ice cream, grabbed a heaping spoonful, then slid it into my mouth.

"Yeah, you shouldn't waste time with people that mean you no good. My mom always says that."

Any good feelings I had morphed into anger at the mention of my mother's name.

Still, I managed a smile and said, "You two seem to get along really well."

"We do."

"What kind of mother was she when you were growing up?" I asked. Partly to dig for information and partly because I needed to understand why she shifted from not wanting a family, to blending into someone else's, to creating a new one.

A nostalgic expression crossed his face. "She's been the best. She never made me feel like a stepchild. I took my real mother's death really hard and I wasn't the best when my dad married Sarah, but she never turned her back on me. She loved me through my rebellion."

She never turned her back.

I contemplated just telling him everything right there, busting this illusion he had of his "mother." Ultimately, I decided against it. Instead I just said, "So where did you say she was from?"

He paused like he was thinking. "I think she's from Atlanta. Both her parents are dead and she's an only child who grew up in foster care. So we're really her only family."

At least she didn't lie about her parents being dead, I thought.

"All I know is I was a handful as a teenager and I gave my

dad grief. Having Mom around grounded me. It made me feel like part of a family. Then Sunny came along and she was just the light of everyone's lives."

I struggled to maintain my composure. The pain in my heart was palpable. "Yeah, your mom seems really loving with Sunny."

"That's the understatement of the decade. That's her little princess. She loved me, but something about having a daughter made her feel complete."

That made my blood boil. Just that easy, she'd found another little princess.

My phone rang. Again. This had to be Trent's thirtieth time calling me since I'd left Raleigh. April had called him and cursed him out. Apparently, Symone hadn't even told him that she'd bumped into me.

I picked up my phone and pressed IGNORE. I made a mental note to block his number, but the phone rang again.

"Is that him?" Alex said when I didn't answer. "Your ex?"

"Yes. He's been calling like crazy."

"You know what? You should answer, tell him off, and tell him to leave you alone," Alex said.

I didn't want to hear anything Trent had to say because if he tried to blame me, this was not going to be pretty. But when my phone rang again, I knew Trent wasn't giving up. I snatched up the phone and pressed ACCEPT.

"What do you want?" I snapped. "Why aren't you off screwing Symone?"

"I'm so glad you picked up," he said, his voice filling with relief. "I can explain."

"Oh, this is explainable?"

"Yes," he began.

"Did you or did you not have sex with Symone?"

"I-I . . ."

"Yes or no. That's the only answer." My voice was calm now.

He sighed, then said, "Yes, but—"

"I'm not interested in hearing anything else you have to say. Lose my number, Trent." I slammed the phone back down and turned off the ringer.

Alex gave me a comforting smile. "Good. Do you know his number by heart?"

I shrugged, trying my best to mask the pain. "Who knows any number by heart?" I said.

Alex took my phone. I watched as he opened the contact info on Trent's number and pressed BLOCK, then DELETE.

Deleting Trent's number was so final. Of course, it would be easy to get it back, but just the move should give me some type of closure. At least I hoped it would.

Alex leaned in and gathered up our empty ice cream containers and spoons. "I'm going to let you get some rest. Plus, I need to get to work. But I'm going to check on you later. If you need me, I'll drop everything and get right back over here."

My hand went to his cheek. "You really are a sweetheart. And Kara is a fool to let you get away."

He looked away, but not before I saw a twinkle in his eyes. "What?" I asked.

"I . . . well, maybe I shouldn't say anything since, you know, you just caught your ex."

I playfully pushed his shoulder. "Boy, you'd better tell me."

His grin was wide as he said, "You were right about Kara hating to see us together. She called and told me how much she missed me and I went by her place and well . . ." He looked away as his grin grew even wider.

"Shut the front door!" I exclaimed. "You two hooked up?"

He nodded, his excitement mirroring a child on Christmas morning. "I mean, she tried to play it off that it didn't mean anything, but she came to me."

"Oh, Alex, I'm so happy for you."

Alex smiled and squeezed my hand. "I'm so glad we're friends."

"Me, too," I said.

I really was. Maybe now we could stay friends—at least until he found out I was his stepsister. I had no idea just how he would take that news.

CHAPTER 31

I'd had enough. I'd lost my man and still hadn't done what I'd come to Atlanta to do. That was going to change. Today.

This wasn't where or how I planned to have an in-depth conversation with my mother. But I couldn't think of a better place—in front of people who admired her.

I had come to the school like she requested, only I was a little later than I had planned. I had no idea I was going to walk into a crowded cafeteria.

My mother and I spotted each other at the same time. She made a beeline in my direction, like she was trying to ward off any impending trouble.

"B-Brooke. I thought you would be here earlier?"

"I got tied up. I didn't know if you'd still be here, and since I don't have my own mother's phone number . . ." I let my words trail off as I glanced around the room. "What's this?"

"A PTA meeting," she replied. "I was hoping we would've had a chance to talk before this started . . ."

Before she could finish, a woman with a head full of gray hair approached us.

"Excuse me," she said to me before turning to my mother. "Mrs. Ford, we really need to get started. The PTA president is ready." She grabbed my mother's hand to pull her away before she could say anything.

My mother, in turn, grabbed my arm. "Please don't leave," she whispered. I didn't respond as the woman dragged her to the stage.

I sat through the God-awful, boring meeting for twenty minutes. My mother hadn't taken her eyes off me. So I'm sure she'd seen me roll my eyes in disgust as the PTA president praised all of "the good work of their esteemed principal." Finally, I'd had all that I could take. I felt like I was going to suffocate, so I stood, stepping over people as I scurried out of the room.

I thought about acting a fool, calling my mother out in front of all these people, but it wasn't even about that anymore. I just wanted to hear her out and put an end to this obsession. My heart couldn't take any more heartbreak. I would just call her and meet somewhere to talk. I crossed over the two people next to me and left. I had just made it to the double doors when I heard, "Brooke."

I stopped and slowly turned toward the sound of my mother's voice.

I folded my arms and glared at her.

"Obviously, you want to talk to me, so why do you keep running?"

I let out a maniacal laugh. "It must be in my blood."

She looked down the hall. The gray-haired lady from earlier was peering down the hall. "Can we step in my office?" my mother said.

I didn't want to, but I needed to hear her excuse. I followed her down the hall and into her office.

"First, let me say, I'm so sorry to hear about Jacob," she said once we were inside her office. "He really was a good man, he just wasn't the man for me." She motioned for me to sit. When I refused, she sat behind her desk and continued talking.

"I had a tumultuous childhood and when I was twenty, I got caught up in some trouble. I stole his wallet from his car when he ran into the grocery store and I used his credit cards. When I was eventually caught, instead of pressing charges, your father agreed to let me volunteer at a youth center he worked at. I was just a young woman and I felt indebted. And before I knew it, we were in a relationship. I wanted to be a dancer. That's all I wanted. I didn't want to be a wife or a mother."

"Oh, it's obvious you didn't want to be a mother," I spat.

"But that's all Jacob talked about," she continued, ignoring my interruption.

She kept talking as if I hadn't said anything and she had been wanting to get this story off her chest for years.

"Your father gave me hope of a better life. He *gave* me a better life, a life I had never known. We married a year after meeting, and a year later, you were born. I assumed the motherly urge would kick in automatically. And the day you were born and they put you on my chest, I waited for the instinct to engulf me. I wanted to enjoy gazing at you for hours at a stretch. I wanted to feel that instant bond." She inhaled, exhaled, then wiped her tears. "But nothing happened. There was no overwhelming urge to nurture or protect. For the longest, I had mixed guilt and distress. I felt I didn't have the genetic equipment necessary to cope with motherhood. I was totally unprepared for the relentlessness of looking after babies. Eventually, I decided that I was just lacking that maternal gene."

"Cry me a river," I said, unmoved by her soliloquy. "Every day some woman doesn't plan to get pregnant and she does and she deals with it."

"The only reason I married your father was because we thought he couldn't have kids," she said matter-of-factly. "And then out of the blue, I ended up pregnant. I was mortified."

She had no idea how much her words were piercing me. But I refused to show it.

"Jacob saw it as a miracle." Nostalgia had taken over. She spoke my father's name with a fondness that contradicted her actions. And then, she added, "And I saw it as the end."

"At least my daddy loved me," I said, my voice shaking.

"I loved you, too," she replied. "I just didn't know how to be a good mother. I grew up not being wanted by either drug-addicted parent and I spent a large amount of my life bouncing around from house to house trying not to overstay my welcome and not be the burden both of my parents saw me as. So I didn't want children out of fear that I'd be the same way to my children, who didn't ask for that life. And then I had you and I had massive reservations toward being the mother you needed."

"You figure it out," I said, slamming my hand on her desk. "You don't leave."

Sadness swept over her. "My mother didn't love me. She told me as much. It is an extremely lonely feeling to be unloved by a parent," she continued. "Especially your mother, and for most of my life I kept that secret from nearly everyone I knew.

I didn't want you to feel that. And then," she paused, "on top of that, I felt suffocated. I felt obligated to your father. I didn't love him like I should've. I was incapable of that type of love."

I rolled my eyes at her words. She didn't seem fazed as she continued. "When I started feeling resentment at you, at Jacob, at his mother who was always around, I just wanted out."

"So you decided to just up and leave?"

"I wasn't thinking clearly. I just needed to get out because I was dying. I had every intention of coming back."

"Whatever," I said.

She stood, then stepped around the desk, coming closer like she desperately wanted me to believe her.

"I did plan to come back. And then I moved to New York. And I got the backup dancing gig with Mariah and I had never been happier. And then, when I finally came back and tried to see you, Jacob wouldn't let me. He said as far as he was concerned, I was dead to the both of you."

More tears fell and this time, I didn't wipe them away. "So you just gave up. You didn't think your child was worth fighting for?"

"Your father told me that you were happy and that you had moved on and my return would only disrupt that."

"I wasn't happy," I said. "I was dying inside."

She lowered her head in shame.

"You convinced yourself that I was happy," I said. "That I was better off, but it was only to ease your guilt. All of which I think is a lie anyway because then you came to Atlanta and started the family you say you didn't want."

She looked away, ashamed. "I was much more mature, older and wiser, when I met my husband. And I grew into motherhood by being a mother to Alex."

"Meanwhile, just screw your real child, right? She couldn't have used this more mature, older wiser woman who was finally ready to be a mother, right?" My sarcasm was on full throttle.

She sighed as a light tap came from the other side of the door.

"Mrs. Ford, is everything all right? Are you coming back to the meeting?"

"Look, I really need to get back into the meeting," she said. "Let's finish this tomorrow. Can you come over tomorrow to my house? Please?"

I immediately tensed up, but then she said, "Alex is going out of town with Anthony on a fishing trip and it will give us a chance to finish and I can answer anything you want."

Part of me was done with my mother. The dreams of mother-daughter bonding were gone. But the part of me that swam in the river of revenge couldn't quite let this go. That's why I said, "Fine. I'll hear you completely out. Just know, I'm not here for your lies."

She hugged me, and though I refused to remove my arms from my side, she said, "I will answer any questions you have."

I believed her. I just didn't know at this point what difference it would even make.

CHAPTER 32

Sarah Ford didn't know the depths of my pain. But by the time the night was over, she would. When Anthony texted me last night and confirmed that he was going out of town with his son, I figured it would be the perfect opportunity to take my mother up on her dinner offer.

I'd texted Anthony before I left home just to make sure he was indeed out of town with Alex because I didn't need him popping up. And based on his flirtatious, "Hello, Beautiful," text this morning, my mother had continued her lie and not come clean.

I was tired and I wanted to finish that conversation once and for all. That's why, though I was once again late, I was standing at her front door, summoning up all of my inner strength, waiting on my mother to open it.

"I didn't think you were going to show," my mother said as she opened the front door. She was wearing an apron, a dish towel in her hand. The picture of domestic tranquility.

"You probably hoped I didn't show," I replied.

She took a deep breath. "You know I really would like for us to get off on the right foot."

"I just came to hear you out."

She sighed again, then stepped aside to let me in.

"Sunny," my mother called out.

"Yes, Mommy." She came skipping over to us. "Hey, you're the lady that was with my brother."

"Yes, that's me." I smiled. As much as I wanted to feel some type of animosity, I couldn't. This wasn't her fault.

"I forgot your name."

"I'm Mona." I cut my eyes at my mother.

"Nice to meet you again, Miss Mona. I'm Sunny."

"Are you sure you're not Cloudy?"

Sunny frowned, then burst into a huge grin. "Ohhhh, I get it. Sunny, cloudy. You're funny."

"So I've been told," I said.

My mother smiled like she was enjoying the banter between her daughters. "I'm going to go check on dinner and then we'll talk."

I nodded.

"You can help me color!" Sunny announced as she slid onto the floor in front of the sofa and pulled out a box of crayons and her coloring book and set them on the coffee table.

"That sounds like a plan," I said.

Sunny and I colored for a few minutes before she said, "Why do you like my brother?" Her doe eyes were wide as she looked in my direction.

The animosity I felt at this child who was living my life raged inside me, but my heart wouldn't allow me to be mean.

"Your brother and I are just friends. But he's a sweet guy. Don't you think so?"

"Sometimes. But sometimes . . ." She let her words trail off.

"Sometimes what?" I asked.

She shook her head. "Mommy said if I can't say anything nice, I shouldn't say anything at all." I couldn't make out the look on her face. She almost looked scared.

I cringed as a memory of my mother telling me that as a little girl flashed through my mind.

"But Alex can be mean," she said, snapping my attention back to her.

I relaxed and smiled. "All brothers are mean at one time or another."

"My mommy said you're way too old for him." She kept drawing; her innocence was so refreshing.

"I'm not that much older than your brother," I replied. "But we're just friends." I pointed to my picture. "Should her dress be pink or brown?"

"Pink," she said. "Princesses don't wear brown!"

"Oh." I exchanged my brown crayon for a pink one.

The house phone rang and Sunny jumped up to answer it. "Hello . . . Yes, please hold."

I couldn't help but admire how mannerable she was.

"Mommy, telephone!" she called out.

My mother entered the room, smiled at me, then took the phone from Sunny.

"Hi, this is Sarah." She listened to the person on the other end of the phone, then her smile slowly faded, morphing into shock. "Are you serious?" she said into the phone. "I . . . I don't know what to say . . . No . . . I understand . . . Okay, thank you for the consideration."

"Mommy, what's wrong?" Sunny said as soon as she hung up. "You look like that was bad news."

"It was," she muttered, still in a daze. "That was the people about my CNN award." She looked at me like a million thoughts were swirling through her head. "They rescinded my award."

Her voice cracked as she stared at me. "Can I talk to you in the kitchen, please?"

I didn't reply, just stood to follow her in the kitchen.

"What?" I asked.

"Do you know anything about this? The producer said they'd gotten some new information and no longer thought I'd be a good fit. What did you do?"

I folded my arms. "How do you know I did anything?"

"You were a conniving little girl and I see nothing has changed."

Her words caught me completely off guard. "Are you serious? How dare you?"

"Why would you do that?" she cried. "I know you told them something. That's why you came back, right? To ruin my life? That award meant the world to me. You didn't want anything from me. You just wanted to hurt me!"

I threw my head back and bucked my eyes in shock. How quickly she had turned. "Just, wow," I said. "Maybe you lost your award because everyone is running around here like you're so great. Maybe they need to know the truth."

"Is that what you came here for?" she repeated.

I stared at her in disbelief.

"What are you doing, Brooke? What is it you want from me?"

I glared at her.

"You want me to suffer? You want to ruin my life? Is it money?" she asked, stomping over to her purse and pulling out her wallet. "I don't have a lot, but I can give you something.

Will that make you feel better? Or will you not be happy until you've destroyed everything I love?"

Talk about being insulted. "I don't need or want your money," I hissed.

"Then what do you want?" Her voice was shaking as if she was on the verge of a breakdown.

"I want you to hurt like you hurt me and my daddy!" I shouted. No, that hadn't been what I'd come here to say, but since we were taking a stroll down bitter lane, I might as well buckle up and prepare for the ride. "You broke his heart, our heart. Then you just started over."

"I'm sorry."

"There will never be enough sorrys to make up for what you've done."

Her anger was subsiding. Now she was in justification mode. "You have to understand what kind of position I was in."

"I don't have to understand anything. I don't care about your sob story." I headed into the living room. So much for dinner. I didn't even say goodbye to Sunny as I stomped toward my car. I had all I needed from my mother. Her response just now had told me all I needed to know.

My mother followed me out. "What are your intentions with Alex?" she asked as I neared my car.

That caused me to stop just feet from the door. I laughed as I turned toward her. I wanted to tell her that was the least of her concerns. Instead I just said, "That's why you had me come over here? You're worried about your *son*?"

"I just . . . I don't want . . . Alex is sensitive. He's sweet, but you just don't understand. I don't want him hurt. And I'm trying to figure out what your intentions are. I mean, are you out to destroy my family?"

"I don't give a damn about your family," I sneered. "If I wanted you destroyed, you'd already be destroyed."

"Are you in love with Alex?"

I couldn't help but laugh again. "I don't want Alex. I just wanted to infiltrate your world."

"So you used him?"

"He'll get over it."

"Brooke, you're playing a dangerous game. I understand you're mad at me, but don't involve him. I'm begging you. Don't do this, Brooke. Alex is fragile," she said. "Please don't drag him into our drama."

I raised an eyebrow at her. "Oh, we have drama?"

"What do you want? Do you want me to say I'm sorry? Because I am. Do you want a relationship, because I would love that." She glanced back over her shoulder. "Ju-just not like this. Just give me time to explain to my family."

If I didn't think I could get any angrier at this woman, I was wrong.

"You are something else!" I screamed at her.

"Please lower your voice."

"Why? Because you're worried about your precious daughter hearing that you're a fraud?"

Sunny must've been listening because she stepped out on the front porch. "Mommy, is everything okay?"

"Okay, obviously, this wasn't a good idea," my mother said. "It's probably a good idea if you leave."

Sunny moved next to my mother. "Are you okay, Miss Mona?"

Her soft words were the only thing that saved me from descending into a full-blown rage. "I'm sorry, Sunny," I said.

"Yeah, I'm very sad. So, yeah, I should leave." My voice was much calmer now.

I flashed one last hateful look at my mother, then I got in my car and pulled off.

This time, however, there were no tears.

CHAPTER 33

I didn't have a reason *not* to do it.

Trent had driven me to it.

My mother had driven me to it.

And right about now, I was going to get satisfaction in the form of revenge.

When Anthony had told me he had an Urban League reception he had to attend, he didn't waste any time asking me to come as well.

Now here I was mingling with a bunch of folks I didn't know, trying to pretend I didn't notice Anthony's lustful gaze.

It took only a few minutes until he excused himself and made his way over to me.

"Hello, Meredith," Anthony said, not bothering to acknowledge the other people I was talking to.

"Hi there," I said, excusing myself from the group of irrelevant people I'd been holding court with. "How was D.C.?"

Anthony broke out into a wide smile. "It was great. Just took a fishing-slash-business trip with some friends. Got some big things in the works. Glad you came."

"Glad you invited me."

We made small talk, but I could tell he wasn't interested in anything I was talking about.

"So, aren't you ready to get out of here?" he asked, leaning in and whispering in my ear.

"And do what?" I asked, my tone inviting.

"We could, umm, we could go back to your place and have a drink and you could tell me all about your plans for the PR project," he said.

I released a flirtatious giggle. "Oh, the project, huh?"

"Yep." Anyone paying us any attention would have no problem figuring out what he wanted from me. "Where do you live?"

"In some condos near downtown. Peachtree Estates."

"Oh, those are nice. My friend was the architect on them; they were subsidized with a city grant. But you know, I never have seen the inside of one," he said, licking his bottom lip.

"Well, what kind of citizen would I be if I didn't let you see firsthand our tax dollars at work? I'll text you the address," I said as I headed toward the door.

I HAD TEXTED ANTHONY my address, and since I'd been home for fifteen minutes now, I was starting to think he'd changed his mind. And since I was hovering between gleefully moving forward and changing my mind myself, I started telling myself that it was probably a good thing he wasn't coming.

And then my doorbell rang.

I glanced through the peephole. Anthony was standing

with a bottle of wine in his hand and apprehension all over his face.

I took a deep breath and opened the door. "Come on in," I said.

He cleared his throat and all traces of nervousness left his face. "I just stopped for wine." He held up the bottle of Pinot Grigio.

I took the bottle and stepped aside for him to enter. "Have a seat and I'll get something to open the wine."

Inside the kitchen, I grabbed the electric wine opener, opened the bottle, then took the bottle with two glasses into the living room.

Anthony was standing right where I left him. I stared at him for a moment and we held our glances, until he looked away. Then I set the wine and glasses on the table and sauntered over to the sofa.

"Come on," I purred, taking his hand. I was in full seduction mode. "Have a seat."

He settled onto the sofa, though he sat on the edge. "So, tell me about these big things you handled in D.C.," I said, while I lowered myself onto the couch next to him. I popped the cork on the wine and poured us both a glass.

"Nothing I can really talk about just yet. But it could mean big news for our city."

I handed him his glass, set mine on the coffee table, and reached for his suit jacket. "I can't wait to hear all the details. Here, let me put these magic hands to use. I used to be a masseuse when I was in college. So come on, and relax," I teased. And then, as I rolled his jacket from his shoulders, I whispered, "You don't need to be scared of me."

After I helped him slip the jacket off, I pointed to the ottoman. It took him a moment to move, but his hesitation didn't concern me. When he sat on the ottoman, my fingertips grazed his shoulders and he tensed.

"Relax," I whispered.

I squeezed his shoulder blades and it took only seconds for him to melt beneath my touch.

I said a silent prayer of gratitude for that six months as a masseuse in college.

Moving my fingers to his neck, I said, "Oh yeah. You're really tense. Do you ever get massages?" I asked, kneading my knuckles into his shoulders.

"No," he moaned. "I just don't have time."

"You have to make time," I said. "These knots are out of control."

Within a few minutes, his moans began to sound like a song. "Ummmm. That feels so good."

"I told you I'm a master at this." I reached over, picked up his glass of wine, and handed it to him. "Sip."

He didn't sip. He turned the whole glass up.

"A tad thirsty, are we?" I chuckled. For someone who was so suave in his flirting, Anthony Ford was acting like this was uncharted territory for him.

He laughed as he set the glass down, then reached for the bottle for a refill. I was a little shocked at his nervousness. Maybe I'd been wrong. Maybe he'd been an all-flirt-and-no-action type of guy. "No, I just needed a drink."

It was the way he sipped and the way he relaxed that made me decide it was time to take my professional massage to the next level. From his neck, I let my fingers tickle a trail down his back.

"Gosh. You have knots in here that are like small plums,"

I said, though I felt nothing. "I'm surprised that you haven't been to the doctor. You are all worked up. Here, let me get in here good." Pressing my chest against his back, I reached around to the front of his shirt, but before I could touch the first button, his hand gripped mine.

"Umm, maybe you shouldn't." His voice was soft and unsure.

"It's just a massage," I said, letting my whisper match his. "Relax."

It took a moment before he dropped his hand away and I stepped in front of him. I kept my eyes away from his as I unbuttoned his shirt and let it fall from his shoulders.

Not bad for a fifty-three-year-old man. But nothing that would have turned me on——on a regular day.

Still, I said, "Wow, you look good."

That brought a smile to his face.

"But business is business," I said, fanning myself. "Whew!" Then I returned to the massage. "Do you work out?" I said in between kneads.

"If you count walking from my car to my office." He moved his head in a circle, savoring the feeling. "But that's just another thing I don't have time for."

"Well, I can't tell."

"Oh, you're being way too nice."

"I'm only speaking the truth."

For minutes I squeezed and kneaded, and when he was totally loose, I said, "You know what? I can't really get into it in this dress. Let me get comfortable so I can really work these knots out. Here, have another drink." I handed him the wine bottle, then sashayed into the bedroom, letting my hips sway as much as I could, knowing his eyes were on me.

The bedroom was in a direct line to the living room. With just a turn of his head, Anthony could have watched me. And when I turned around, his eyes were still on me.

But with a coy smile, I closed the door, then laughed once I was out of his sight. This was so easy.

I had already laid out my red slinky skater dress and slipped into it. In front of the mirror I adjusted the straps, making sure my boobs were lifted, my cleavage was prominent, and the dress was long enough to cover my butt yet short enough to show my thighs. I felt a sense of excitement. Not because of anything with him, but because revenge was wetting my palate. I'd set the bait. Now I needed to reel him in.

"All right," I said, the moment I opened my bedroom door.

His eyes met mine and the sip of wine that he was about to take was arrested as he held the glass on the edge of his lip.

Moving with a model's stroll, I said, "Let me really work those knots out."

It was as if his eyes were stuck on me. He didn't even blink. "Wow, you're beautiful."

"Thank you," I said, immediately moving behind him before he changed his mind. But after just a couple of seconds, I said, "I'm not getting as deep as I want to; let's move back to the couch and you can stretch out."

He stood, but he hesitated. "I think . . . I mean . . . I'm m-much better now," he stammered.

Of course he was, but I wasn't finished. "Nonsense," I said, keeping my voice light. "Will you come on?"

His steps were slow, timid, but he finally lay across the sofa, head down, eyes closed.

I felt the victory and I straddled him, pressing the center

of me into his lower back. I hadn't even touched him and he moaned.

The moves were perfunctory now; I'd done my job, his body was nothing more than a noodle. But my touch made him groan and moan, filling the air with the desire for me that he hadn't yet acknowledged.

I leaned forward and with my hands still moving on his back, I grazed his neck with my lips. He surprised me—there was no resistance, just deeper sighs.

When I leaned back, he turned over. Our eyes locked and without saying a word, I told him what I wanted. I wanted to lose myself in him. And for a moment—this moment—I just wanted him to make me forget the pain of Trent and my mother. Anthony pushed himself up, brought me closer to him, and when he covered my lips with his, he told me what he wanted, too.

I pressed myself into him and now his moans were filled with his yearning. In just two seconds I was out of my dress. Less than thirty seconds after that, he was out of his pants.

Then I was the one lying on my back. Anthony took over. And any love he had for my mother was momentarily replaced with unyielding lust for me.

CHAPTER 34

$\mathcal{I}$f sex was a helluva drug, guilt was some kind of hangover.

And I'd been racked with guilt. I hated that I was, but I was.

As much as I wanted my mother to hurt, she would never know what I had done. I'd resolved that last night. While the sex—as lackluster as it was—had brought me momentary satisfaction, I woke up this morning feeling like crap.

I'd slept with a married man.

I'd slept with a married man who had slept with my mother.

What the hell was wrong with me?

My phone vibrated, shaking away my guilt and snapping me away from my drama and back to Nina's. Her record label was threatening to drop her unless she issued a public apology for the boyfriend-dousing incident, but she was adamantly refusing to do so.

The phone continued vibrating. I ignored it and said, "So what do you guys think of the statement?" Both Nina J. and her assistant, Amiya, had been reading over the statement, which I had spent the last two hours crafting.

"It sounds good to me," Amiya said.

"It sounds like a load of crap to me." Nina tossed the paper back onto my desk. Then she picked up a copy of *Essence* magazine and began casually flipping through the pages.

I let out a heavy sigh. "Please, Nina. Is this worth losing your career?"

"I'll bounce back." She didn't bother looking up. Her nonchalant attitude about something so serious was working my nerves. Amiya shook her head, giving me a look to know that Nina J. was my problem now.

"You have worked too hard to build your name," I said. "Just give the apology. Everyone will know you don't really mean it."

"Then why give it, if I don't mean it?" She didn't even look up as she spoke.

"To play nice," I pleaded.

She closed her magazine and looked at me. Her green contacts were off-putting, but other than that, and her fiery blond hair, she was one of the most gorgeous women I'd ever seen. "That's what's wrong with America," Nina said. "We let everyone do us wrong."

My phone vibrated again.

"Do you need to get that?" Nina J. asked. "Because whoever it is ain't letting it go."

"I'm sorry. Give me a minute." I pressed ACCEPT on the number, which I didn't recognize.

"We really need to finish talking," my mother said. "Please don't hang up."

"How'd you get my number?" My hand shook, wondering if she knew about me and Anthony.

"Alex."

I turned my chair around, away from Nina and Amiya. Of course my mother didn't know. He wouldn't have told her. "We're finished talking. You said what you needed to say. I don't have anything else to say to you." I tried to keep my tone as professional as possible.

"Brooke, I understand you don't want to have anything to do with me but we can't end things like that."

I cut her off. "That's the way you would like it, right? For me to just go away and not upset your perfect little lie?" I remembered my clients and quickly said, "I will call you later." Then slammed the phone down.

"Hmph, seems like I'm not the only one that needs to throw some boiling water on someone," Nina said.

I rubbed my temple. "I'm so sorry about that. That is so unprofessional."

She dropped the magazine in her lap. "Girl, no." Nina J. leaned forward and for the first time since she stepped into my office, I had her undivided attention. "For real, though. That's the problem. We let people do us wrong and we don't do anything about it. High road, my ass. We all can't be Michelle when-they-go-low, we-go-high Obama. Sometimes you have to get in the gutter with folks so they'll think twice before hurting you again." She paused. "So what was that about?"

I was a professional. I was not about to have this discussion with a client, let alone one I just met. So I just said, "Family drama."

Nina was relentless. "Obviously, whoever that was on the phone has pissed you off. What are you doing about it?"

"I'll have a discussion with her later."

"A *discussion*?" Nina J. shook her head like I was a charity case. "Sometimes you need to back your words up with some actions."

If only she knew.

"Nina . . ."

"I'm just saying. My boyfriend screwed my stylist and you think I was supposed to let that slide? Plus, throwing that hot water made me feel so much better. Try it. You might like it."

Amiya said, "I've been trying to get through to her. First Peter 3:9, says, 'Do not repay evil with evil or insult with insult. On the contrary, repay evil with blessing, because to this you were called so that you may inherit a blessing.'"

Nina rolled her eyes and waved her off. "Girl, bye. I live by the Muhammad Ali philosophy: You kill my dog, you better hide your cat."

"Revenge is a confession of pain," Amiya said. She seemed wise beyond her years, but it was obvious Nina wasn't trying to hear any of that.

"You know what? I'm not having this conversation with you," I interjected. "Can we get back to business?"

Nina threw up her hands. "Fine if you don't want to talk about it, but I'm telling you, peace of mind is a beautiful thing and sometimes revenge is the only way to get that peace of mind. And then the person that wronged you knows they'd better think twice before doing it again."

I smiled. "Let's take that you-don't-play attitude and channel it into getting you out of this mess."

"Not mess. *Situation*." She stood and threw her three-thousand-dollar Louis Vuitton hobo bag over her shoulder. "But that's what I pay you for. You figure it out. I'm good with that last statement. Come on, Amiya. I need to go to the mall."

I stopped her right before she got to the door. "Nina, thank you for the advice."

"Heed my words. You seem like a sweet chick. But sweet chicks come in last and have nothing but trampled-on feelings to show for it."

I weighed her words as she left. Before he left last night, Anthony had asked to come over again after work today. I'd agreed because at the time I had no idea sleeping with Anthony wouldn't give me the personal satisfaction I had hoped it would. And I couldn't help but wonder if anything ever would.

No. I'd done my dirt. I was ashamed, unsatisfied, and my heart still hurt. So that secret would go with me to my grave.

CHAPTER 35

Revenge is a confession of pain.

The words of Nina J.'s assistant had swirled in my head all day. And now they were front and center, fighting off the desire to run to my mother and beg her to forgive me for what I'd done with her husband and let me back into her heart.

That's the first thought I'd had when I pulled up to my condo and saw my mother sitting in the bistro chair near the front door.

I parked, then slowly made my way up the walkway as my mother's eyes remained on me. I tried desperately to read behind them so I could determine how I needed to approach her.

My mother's voice shook as she said, "Hi. Sorry to just show up here, but I got your address from Alex, too, and well, I just want to talk to you."

No matter how much my heart wanted to be angry, I could only say, "Fine," as I walked past her and unlocked the front door. I was tired. Tired of the games. Of running after her. Tired of the losses. I would hear her out, then I would let her go.

"Thank you for agreeing to talk to me," she said once she had followed me in.

I didn't reply as I removed my jacket and set my purse down.

She didn't bother sitting and just started rambling. "Brookie, I mean, Brooke," she corrected. "I'm so sorry I hurt you. And I understand your anger. But please don't hate me."

I just stared at her. She had the nerve to have tears in her eyes. I couldn't muster up an iota of sympathy.

"I don't expect you to understand why I did what I did," she said.

"Glad you don't expect me to understand, because I never will. Do you have any idea how many tears I shed because I thought you were dead and—"

"That was your father's decision," she said, interrupting me.

I jumped in her face, causing her to flinch. "I told you, you don't get to say anything about my father! He was just trying to help me cope with the fact that my mother threw me away like yesterday's trash."

She took a deep breath. "That's not what I meant. Look, I understand that you're bitter."

I calmed down, took a step back. I did not want to get worked up. "You don't know the half of it."

"Brooke, I really did love you. And your father. In my own way."

"You don't love anything but this fake-ass life you created," I said, exasperated. "After twenty-five years, you finally see me and that was your first concern, whether I was here to let everyone know what a liar you were."

"I know I did not respond correctly when I saw you. It's just, that, well . . . I just freaked out."

My doorbell rang as we faced off. I didn't even think as I headed to the door. I just welcomed the reprieve, hoping it would calm me down. I felt like this was the now-or-never conversation with my mother, and me being all angry and flustered wasn't going to help.

I guess I was flustered because I didn't bother looking out the peephole. I just swung the door open.

And there stood Anthony.

"Hey, sexy," he said, a wide grin over his face.

My stomach turned a backflip. I completely forgot that I had told him he could swing by after work.

He didn't give me time to reply as he took me into his arms and kissed me. All of the reservation he initially felt was gone.

He hugged me as he said, "I've been thinking about you all day. I don't know what kind of magic good stuff you put on me yesterday but . . ."

His words trailed off as his eyes made their way past my shoulder and into the middle of the living room.

"S-Sarah?" he stammered.

He almost knocked me down as he raced over to my mother, who was standing with a look of sheer horror across her face.

"Sarah! Oh, my God. What are you doing here?"

I closed the door, and fought back the bile that was rising in my stomach.

This. I didn't want this.

"No, Anthony," my mother said, her voice quivering as her eyes filled with tears. "No . . . no . . . no. Please, no."

"Baby, I . . . I can explain," he stammered.

Tears spilled from my mother's eyes. "How could you do this?" she cried, looking between the two of us. I wasn't sure which one of us she was talking to.

"No, I can explain, sweetheart. I'm so sorry. It's not how it looks." Every time he reached for her, she jumped away.

"You're sleeping with her?" my mother asked, still in disbelief.

"It's not like that," he pleaded, his voice reeking of desperation.

"I heard you. Just now, I heard you." My mother glared at me. "Why would you do this? How could you be so low-down?"

"What?" I asked, trying to shake off my own shock and horror. Of course she would direct all of her venom at me. I was nothing more to her than an inconvenience from her past.

The anger I had been feeling was back and had become a full raging inferno.

"Are you really asking me that?" I took a couple of steps in her direction. She backed up as if she thought I was about to hit her. "So, now I'm the low-down one?"

Anthony turned to me. "You told me to come over. Was it so you could set me up?"

I spun on him. "No, I told you you could come *back* over after you asked," I corrected. "I had no idea your wife was just going to pop up at my place."

Anthony turned to my mother. "Why are you here?"

The irony of those words brought me momentary satisfaction. I could see the lies churning in my mother's head. I stepped in before she let them come out of her mouth. The come-to-Jesus moment was here.

"Yes, tell him why you're here, Mommy Dearest," I calmly said.

"What?" Anthony said. He looked back and forth between the two of us. "Do you know Meredith?" he repeated, since my mother was still standing there silently sobbing. It was obvious she wasn't going to answer him, so he turned back to me. "Do you know my wife?" he demanded.

"Oh yeah. I know her." I nodded, and folded my arms across my chest. I hated that it had come to this but I was dumbfounded that even up until the last moment, my mother was going to continue to deny me. "She's the first person I ever knew," I said.

Anthony's confusion was on full display now. "Will someone tell me what the hell is going on here?" he shouted.

I kept my eyes focused on my mother. "Shall you explain or should I?"

"You. Slept. With. Her," my mother said, ignoring me. She gazed at her husband. "Why would you do this?" she sobbed. "How could you do this? You promised . . . I thought we had gotten to a good place . . . I thought we had a good marriage."

"We do." He was back to being apologetic. He reached for her and once again, she backed away. "I am so sorry. I will spend my life making this up to you."

"How long have you been having an affair with her?" my mother snapped.

"It was just one time," he cried. "Baby, let's go home and talk about this," Anthony said, deciding to focus all his attention on his wife and forget about me.

Just as my mother had done.

"I've got to get out of here," my mother said, bolting toward the door.

But I wasn't about to let her off that easy. I jumped in front of the front door, blocking it.

"Oh no, ma'am. You're not running away again," I said.

"Little girl, if you don't get out of my way . . ." my mother hissed.

"*Little girl?* Yeah, I was a little girl when you left." I stepped so close to her that our tears could've mixed. "But I'm a grown-ass woman now."

Her shoulders dropped in defeat. Her voice was just above a whisper as she said, "Do you hate me that much, to do something like this?"

"Will somebody tell me what's going on?" Anthony yelled again. "How do you know my wife?"

I kept my eyes on her as I said, "I knew your wife before you knew your wife."

I had felt guilty about my tryst with Anthony. But not anymore. My mother had rejected me for the last, the final time. Now she needed to know pain like I knew pain. Revenge wasn't so bad after all.

I turned to Anthony. "How does it feel to have made love to a mother *and* daughter?"

"Huh?" He looked at my mother. She turned away. "What is she talking about, Sarah?"

"Yeah. Tell him what I'm talking about, Mommy."

He spun on me. "Don't be ridiculous. I don't know what kind of sick game you're playing or why. But my wife only has one child," Anthony said.

I waved a finger at him. "Ahh, ahh, ahh. That's where you're wrong, Deputy Mayor. I'm your wife's *first* child."

His eyes bucked.

"Oh, let me guess, she didn't tell you anything about me?" I asked.

He looked at Sarah, a mixture of shock and hurt across his face. "You had a baby you gave up for adoption? Why didn't you think you couldn't tell me that?"

"Yeah, that story," I tsked. "That's probably how she would have liked to have believed it went, but she didn't give me up for adoption at birth. She abandoned me when I was seven years old."

"What?" he exclaimed, now sounding like a broken record with a chorus of *whats*.

Still, my mother said nothing.

"Yes, your precious perfect woman-of-the-year wife ran out on her husband and child to start a new life. She didn't feel like being bothered with us, so she just discarded us, and let me live all these years thinking she was dead."

"It wasn't like that at all," my mother said, finally finding her voice. Her tone was still just above a whisper, as if all of this had drained her soul.

"This isn't making sense," Anthony said.

"Did you even get a divorce from my father? I mean, are you even legally married to Anthony?" I asked her.

Sarah glared at me through her tears. "I hope you're happy. I hope you got what you wanted."

I moved and opened the door. "If you're hurting, then I'd say I have."

She shook her head, released another heavy sob, then ran out of the door.

The anger and tears and years' worth of bitterness were finally boiling over.

"I don't believe you did this!" Anthony yelled at me before bolting out the door after his wife.

"I don't care what you believe!" I screamed back, slamming the door behind him. "I want that bitch to feel my pain!"

I picked up the three-thousand-dollar vase and threw it against the door. As it crashed and splattered to the ground, I fell to the floor as well, sobbing that while I'd come to do what I wanted to do, the hole in my heart felt wider than ever.

CHAPTER 36

*I*t had been a rough night. I hadn't gone into the office today. After peeling myself off the floor last night, I'd drowned my sorrows in a bottle of tequila. And now I was paying the price. The hangover of all hangovers had what felt like a death grip on my head.

That's why the knocking on my door sounded like a jack-hammer. I stumbled toward the noise, just to make it stop.

"Who is it?" I said through the door.

The banging continued. I looked out the peephole to see Alex. He had that dark look in his eyes so I wasn't about to open the door.

He noticed me through the peephole and just like that, the darkness disappeared. "Hey, it's Alex. I've been out here knocking for ten minutes. I thought maybe you were upstairs and couldn't hear me."

"Ummm, Alex, I'm not feeling too well. Call me later," I said through the door.

"Are you talking to me? I can't hear you." He knocked again and just to get it to stop, I cracked the door.

"Hey Alex," I said, "I feel awful so just call me later."

"I need to talk to you, can I come in? Just for a minute," he asked.

"Alex, I don't think that's a good idea." I knew that I owed him a conversation. I don't know if he knew anything or not. I couldn't tell from the blank expression on his face. But I just couldn't deal with any of it today.

"Why not?" He smiled. "You look like you partied a little too hard last night. I'll make coffee."

"Alex . . ."

"Please?"

I sighed, then stepped aside and let him in. It really had been wrong the way I'd used him, and if he did know who I really was, I owed him an explanation.

"So, what's with the suitcases?" he asked as he stepped in the living room. I vaguely remembered throwing all of my belongings into the suitcases last night. But I must have really been drunk because I didn't remember packing three bags.

"Umm, I'm heading home tomorrow." I massaged my temples, hoping I could will the pounding away.

"And you weren't even going to say goodbye?" Alex asked.

"Of course I was. I'm just . . . I'm just out of it right now."

"Uh, let's get that coffee." He headed into the kitchen. I followed as he started talking about some new book he wanted me to check out. Maybe he didn't know anything. Regardless, it was time that he did.

He put a K-Cup pod in my Keurig, placed a cup under the spout, and pressed START. As the coffee began to brew, Alex took a step toward me. "Brooke, I just wanted to tell you how much you've made a difference in my life. I know I said I was gonna get back with Kara but I can't because I want you so bad."

I pushed him back—hard. "Alex, I already told you I'm not feeling you like that." I groaned because the last thing I felt like was dealing with this.

A slow smirk spread across his face. "Oh yeah, you don't want me. You want my father."

All remnants of my hangover were instantly gone. "Ah, uh, what are you talking about?"

"Don't play me for stupid!" he yelled. "You've been using me, leading me on because you were having an affair with my father."

I took a step back. "Look, Alex, I've never led you on. I've been clear from the jump."

He slammed his palm on the kitchen counter. "Bullshit! You've been playing me and you know what they say when you play with fire, right?" The rage in his eyes scared me.

"Alex, I think you need to leave," I said.

"Ho, I ain't going nowhere."

His words stunned me. "Alex!" I knew that he was losing it so I needed to stay calm.

"Don't 'Alex' me, you home-wrecking tramp. My parents fought all night and now my dad is moving out. They told me everything, including how you weren't ever my friend and were just using me to try and get information on my family."

"I am your friend." My words were slow and calculated. "It's so much more complicated than that. Please, you have to understand."

"No! I don't have to understand anything, except, you

think it's cool to play with people's emotions. You think it's cool to break up someone's family."

I took several steps backward. The insanity in his eyes caused me to look for escape routes. "She broke up my family first," I managed to say.

"Shut up," he snapped. "Not only did you hurt her, but you hurt my dad, and me, and my little sister."

"Alex, what about what she did to me?" I was hoping I could reason with him.

"Guess what? I don't care about you. Since you obviously don't care about anyone else."

To say I was scared would be an understatement. The rage in his eyes, coupled with the frantic gestures he was making, had me terrified.

"I'm sorry about everything, but I really want you to leave."

"Naw, I don't think so." In one svelte move, he snatched a long butcher knife out of the knife rack. "In fact, let me tell you how this is going to play out," he continued. "You're gonna call my mother and tell her you made it all up."

"She was here, Alex," I said, even though it didn't seem like he'd be able to process any rational thoughts. "She heard everything, plus your father admitted to everything."

"Well, tell her you put him up to it!" He snatched my cell phone off the counter and jabbed it at me.

My trying to reason and get him to see things logically was not working so I tried a different approach. "Alex, I like you a lot, but your father—"

"—was seduced by a whore. And you used me to make your seduction plan come to fruition. You probably don't even like books." There was a crazed look dancing in his eyes, once again causing me to tremble.

"Alex."

"Stop calling my name!" His cell phone rang. He pulled it out of his pocket, looked at the screen, then slapped his head. "Ugh."

I was trying to weigh if there was any way I could make a run for the door. But the way he was right now, I didn't think he'd hesitate to kill me.

"Okay, look, here's what I'll do," I reasoned. "I'll just leave town and never return. And you all can just forget you ever met me."

"So you think you'll destroy my family, then just up and leave? Naw, it doesn't work like that."

His phone rang again. I was praying that he would answer. "You'd better keep it shut," he said, before pushing the TALK button.

"Hello!" Alex screamed into the phone. He pointed the knife in my direction as if to tell me not to move. "No, Dad. I told you I was gonna handle it . . . I'm not telling you where I am. Since she's so big on revenge, I'm just going to make her pay."

"Help me, please! He's at my condo!" I screamed.

Alex dropped the phone, then reached over and slapped me harder than I'd ever been hit in my life. The force of his hand knocked me to the floor.

"Didn't I tell you to shut the hell up?" he screamed. "You women don't ever know when to shut up!"

I sniffled as I fought back more tears. "Please, you don't want to hurt me."

He leaned down. "Oh believe me, I do. I just have to figure out the best way. I could plunge this knife into your heart right now, but I think that's too easy." He ran the knife down the center of my chest, the tip piercing the point where my breasts met.

I was taking slow breaths to keep from becoming hysterical.

"Yeah, all the dreams I've had about you and I making love. I think it's a good idea that I make those dreams a reality."

I couldn't say anything. Fear had paralyzed me. "You're not a rapist," I said to him.

"You don't know what I am. Everybody thinks I'm crazy anyway. I can rape you, then just plead insanity."

Images of a frightened Kara flashed through my mind.

"Alex is fragile."

"My brother can be so mean."

"My son is . . . special."

Was Alex crazy for real?

"Oh, my God," I mumbled.

"Even God can't help you now."

"Alex, this doesn't make sense. We're friends."

He was silent, deep in thought, and I wondered what was going through his head. I was just about to try to reason with him when someone started banging on the door.

"Alex, son, open the door!" I heard Anthony yell.

"Ugh, what is he doing here?"

"Help!" I shouted. Alex turned around and once again slapped me.

"Son, please let us in!" Sarah shouted through the door. "It's not worth it."

I could hear two pairs of hands banging on the door.

"They're not going to go away and pretty soon they're going to get the attention of my neighbors," I said from the floor. I was going to die. That's all I could think. If I didn't get away from this maniac, I was going to die.

Alex glared at me, grabbed me by the hair, and dragged me into the living room. "Help!" I yelled. It's like he had super-human strength and no matter how hard I flailed, I couldn't break free.

Alex slammed me against the wall next to the front door. "Go away!" he yelled through the door.

I struggled to pull myself up off the floor.

"Open the door, Alex," Anthony said.

"No. I told y'all I'm not going to let her get away with this."

"Please, son," my mother said.

He took a deep breath, then slowly moved to open the door. As soon as he did, I bolted. I ran to the back bedroom, screaming. I heard Sarah and Anthony calling after Alex. It sounded like he'd taken off right after me but I was running like my life depended on it and didn't look back to be sure.

I locked the bedroom door and slid stuff in front of the door like they do in the movies. I looked around the room, frantic. I'd left my cell phone in the kitchen. Then it dawned on me, my Apple Watch! I immediately hit the phone icon and dialed for help.

"Nine-one-one, what's your emergency?" the operator said.

"Help! He's in my house trying to kill me," I shouted as I scooted a bench in front of my bedroom door. I jumped as Alex banged on the door.

"Ma'am, what's your location?" the dispatcher asked.

"1612 Sagewood Drive, unit 22B. Hurry, he's crazy!" I cried.

"Open this door!" Alex screamed.

I moved into the bathroom and put up a barricade of laundry hampers and everything else I could find in front of the door.

"Ma'am, the police are near. Are you in a safe location?" the dispatcher asked.

"I'm barricaded in the bathroom," I whispered, then yelled toward the door. "You'd better go, the cops are on the way!"

I heard Sarah and Anthony mumbling but I couldn't make out what they were saying and I really didn't care.

"Ma'am, is everything okay? Where are you?" the dispatcher asked.

"I'm locked in my bathroom now, but he's gonna get in. Please, hurry. He has a knife."

"You're not going to get away!" Alex yelled. It sounded like he'd gotten in the bedroom. "I'm gonna make you pay!"

He hit, then kicked the door as I cowered in the corner of the bathtub.

"Ma'am, the police have arrived."

"Tell them to hurry!" I cried.

With every kick, I flinched. With every pound, I cried.

I guess Alex had locked my bedroom door because it sounded like his parents were banging on the door.

"Let us in son!" Anthony yelled.

Just then I heard, "Police, freeze, drop your weapon!"

Alex hit the bathroom door, which crashed open, and I screamed as he lunged at me. I scrambled out of the way and dove farther into the bathtub as I prepared to join my father. I cringed in horror, then, as he raised the knife, a single gunshot pierced the air. Alex stopped, his eyes bucked, then his hand went to his abdomen, which was staining with blood. I cowered in the tub as he slowly fell to the floor.

"Noooooo!" Anthony cried as he raced to his son's side.

Alex's body jerked as he gasped for air. "I'm s-sorry. I just wanted her to pay."

Anthony's wail was joined by Sarah's as Alex's eyes rolled into the back of his head.

CHAPTER 37

··

"*Precious Lord take my hand. Lead me on and let me stand.*" I fought back the tears as the soloist belted out what once was one of my favorite gospel songs. But now I know I'd never be able to listen to this song again without a memory of this service and the role I played in leading to this day.

"*I am tired. I am weak.*"

My eyes scanned the small church. People of all races sat in the pews, and an array of flowers surrounded the cherry-wood casket. I had begun this journey with a funeral and I was ending with one. I would give anything to change both times.

As the soloist wound down, the minister took the stand.

"At this time we'd like anyone who would like to speak to come up. Please keep your comments to two minutes," he said.

The petite elderly lady next to me leaned in. "You wanna go up? You've been sitting back here pretty broken up. It might help you feel better to say something," she said.

I clutched my handful of tissue and vehemently shook my head.

"No pressure, baby," she whispered. "Say goodbye in your own way."

She turned her attention back to the front, where several people had come up to give words of condolences. They talked about being classmates, customers, friends. From the comments, the Alex who showed up at my house last week was not the same man all of these people knew.

I felt a tug at my heart as Alex's ex, Kara, took the stand. She wore all black and her hair was pinned back in a bun, putting her puffy, grief-stricken eyes on full display.

"Hello, everyone," she began, her voice soft and low. It was obvious that it was taking everything inside her to speak. "I didn't think I would have the strength to get up here. As many of you know, I have loved Alex since I met him in the ninth grade and my prayer had always been that one day we would find our way back to each other. Despite his . . . well, despite any issues, we all know that Alex had the most loving heart. He loved hard."

Several people in the audience chuckled.

"Whether it was caring for a stray puppy, me, or"—she looked over at my mother, Anthony, and Sunny—"his loving family, he was fiercely protective." She stood erect. "I am heartbroken because Alex and I were going to try and make things work between us and I was so happy. It is that good side of him that I will choose to remember. It is that side that I will"—her hand went to her stomach as she took a deep breath—"choose to tell our child about." The Ford family flashed pained smiles. It was obvious they had already received this news. "When our child comes into the world, I will let him know how absolutely amazing his father was."

Silent sobs punctuated her speech. Her sister, Jada, rushed

to her side and guided her back to her seat. I was frozen. Alex was going to be a father.

I didn't have long to process that revelation because Anthony took the podium. My mother was by his side. They gripped hands, connecting like they were Siamese twins. I guess grief had united them and taken precedence over betrayal.

Anthony began speaking, his voice hoarse and heavy with grief. "We debated whether to speak, but I wanted to let you know on behalf of our family that we are grateful for the love you all showed Alex and are now showing us. We will never understand why things happened the way that they did." My mother squeezed his arm to give him strength. "My son suffered from borderline personality disorder. He had been doing great, and we were so proud of his progress. That's why we are starting a scholarship in his honor to help other young people like himself. We hope that you will help us continue to raise awareness of this mental illness that often goes undiagnosed." He inhaled, then blew a long breath. "Please keep us in your prayers." He turned toward the casket. "To my beloved son, I will see you in Heaven." And then Anthony let loose a sob that resonated at my core.

I had been sitting in the back. The absolute last row. I'd worn a black hat and sunglasses and I prayed that Anthony, or my mother, didn't see me. I knew that I shouldn't be here, but I had to. I'd gone to the bookstore to get funeral details. I'd been absolutely devastated at the pain I'd caused.

My mother glanced at the rear of the church as they made their way back to their seats. I quickly buried my head in the program, praying that she didn't see me. When Anthony let out a wail, crying, "My son, my son!" I couldn't take it anymore. I stood, excused myself as I stepped over people on my row, and bolted from the church. Outside, I stopped short of getting in my car and heading up I-85 back to Raleigh. If I never set foot in Atlanta again, it would be too soon. But I couldn't do that until I'd faced them—Anthony and my mother. Faced them and told them that I was sorry.

I was pacing the sidewalk in front of the church when I noticed my phone vibrating. I pulled it out of my purse. April had once again been blowing up my cell. I finally answered.

"Hello."

"Oh, my God. Brooke, I've been so worried about you. I've been calling all morning."

"I just left the funeral," I said.

"Are you okay?" she asked.

"No," I said, the tears starting up again. "But I guess I will be."

"Grandma is a nervous wreck. We all are," April said.

I held my breath, hoping and praying that she would say Trent had been going out of his mind as well. Right now I would give anything for his comforting arms. But my cousin simply said, "The two of us almost got in the car and drove down there."

"I'm okay. I'm packed up." As much as I'd wanted to just leave after everything that went down at my condo, I had to close out the business in the Atlanta office. I'd fast-tracked everything and hired a publicist within a week. I had to get out of Atlanta and planned to do that as soon as this was over.

"Have you talked to Aunt Sarah?" April asked.

"No. I'm outside the church. I'm waiting now. The services are about to wrap up."

"I don't know if that's a good idea," April said. "Maybe you should just come back and then go back and talk to her some other time."

"I have to do this. I have to talk to her. Tell both of them how sorry I am and then I'm going to come back and hopefully I can talk to Trent and we can . . . I don't know, we both messed up and maybe we can fix things."

"Brooke," April said, her tone sympathetic, "I don't know how to tell you this. I don't even know if now is the time, but I don't want you to come back with your hopes up."

I stopped pacing and said, "Why?"

"Trent and Symone are an item now. They're together."

My heart. I didn't think there were any cracks left in my heart. But I felt them nonetheless.

"Don't worry about that right now, though," she said.

"So, I lost him? I really lost him?"

"We're not going to worry about that right now," April repeated. "Right now we're focused on you and getting you back here."

My hand trembled as I held the phone. "Trent told me. He told me I was going to lose him and for what? I just . . ."

"Just come home."

I took a deep breath. "Okay. Hey, I'll call you once I get on the road. They're letting out," I said as I noticed people filing out of the church. "And I want to catch Sarah before she leaves."

"Okay. Be sure and call me."

I hung up the phone and made my way to the front. I nearly collapsed as they wheeled Alex's body out to the car. My mother and Anthony stood behind the hearse as they lifted it into the back, then closed the door. I eased up to stand by the family car.

"Sarah," I softly said as they headed to the car.

They both stopped, and for the first time, I saw the devastation in Sunny's eyes. I hadn't even thought about what this was doing to this precious little girl. Anthony glared at me. "Why are you here?"

Why are you here?

That had become the running theme of my life.

My mother's hand went to his arm. He shot me the most hateful expression. "I hope you're happy," he said. "Is this what you wanted? My son dead? You got your revenge, right? You made your mother pay, right? That's all that matters, right?"

My mother rubbed his back. "Anthony, go wait in the car." Her voice was somber. I trembled as people stared at me. My mother just looked at me.

"I'm so sorry," I said.

The look of hate on his face, and of disappointment in my mother's eyes, broke my heart. "I can't do this. I *won't* do this." He grabbed Sunny's hand and all but dragged her off.

"I never meant for any of this to happen," I whispered after they were gone.

She nodded. "Yeah, none of us did." She dabbed at the tears coming down from her cheeks. "Brooke, all you had to do was come to me. Talk to me. And we could have worked through this. All of the sneaking around, with Alex, with Anthony, trying to get info on me wasn't necessary. You could have just come to me and asked."

I swallowed, fought back the tears. Why didn't I just go to her and ask? Why had I let revenge consume me?

"I did come to you. And when you didn't recognize me, when you rejected me again . . ."

My words trailed off and I expected her to protest, but she simply nodded her understanding.

Finally, I said, "So what now?"

She was pensive. "I don't know. A lot of damage has been done. I just don't . . ."

"It's okay," I said, trying to summon up my own strength. "I've been alone this long. The rest of my life won't hurt."

That looked as if it stung, but it didn't change her mind. "I'm sorry. I'm not saying never, because I bear a large part of this blame. But right now we need to heal individually. And maybe . . ." She let her words trail off.

There was nothing else for me to say. All of the bitterness and anger I had was gone, and right now "maybe" was all I had.

"Okay." I nodded. I don't know why but I desperately wanted her to lean in, to hug me, to tell me that she forgave me. I would tell her that I forgave her and we'd work on our relationship. But she simply squeezed my arm and said, "Take care of yourself," and then turned and walked away.

I dabbed the tears as I headed to my car, and as the Atlanta skyline disappeared in my rearview mirror, I could only think the revenge had so not been worth it. In seeking Sarah, I'd lost myself. And everything that mattered. Now it was time to reclaim me. And if a relationship with my mother was ever meant to be—it would be.

I slipped my sunglasses back on, changed my radio to the gospel station, and headed home.

EPILOGUE

....

Eighteen Months Later

This was not the way my story was supposed to end.

I'd sacrificed my future trying to recapture my past. I did have a relationship with my mother now, but it was nowhere near what I had dreamed of. We were like old friends, reconnecting, getting to know one another all over again.

The problem was I didn't want any more friends. I wanted a mother.

In time, I guess.

For now, I had to focus on *being* a mother.

"Ma-ma."

I smiled at my baby girl, Nicolette. The joy of my life. My saving grace. She was pointing to her stuffed poodle, which had fallen on the ground.

"Mommy has it," I said, picking it up and handing it back to her in her stroller.

"So, it looks like everything is in there."

I snapped my attention back to Trent, who was standing in front of me going through Nicolette's diaper bag.

"As if it wouldn't be," I said.

"I know, I know. You're a great mother," Trent replied. "I just wish you understood that I'm a great father, too."

I released a heavy sigh. "I know that. Or else she wouldn't be going with you." I handed him her jacket. "Make sure you give her the medicine in the yellow container and please, no sweets."

"Brooke, I know how to take care of my daughter," Trent said.

I glanced over his shoulder. The sight of Symone sitting in his car made me ill.

His *wife,* Symone.

I'd love to say that I walked over, spoke, chatted about how her day was, but I wasn't there yet. Lord knows it was going to take a lot of prayer to get me there.

Just before she and Trent had gotten married six months ago, she'd tried to come and talk to me. I didn't have anything to say to her. I just asked that she didn't mistreat my child.

"You know me better than that," she had said.

"No," I'd replied, "obviously I didn't know you at all."

Those had been the last words I'd uttered to her.

Despite her continued efforts, I couldn't forgive her betrayal. That pain ran deep and I didn't have any room in my heart to heal it. Maybe someday.

But since today wasn't that day, I turned my attention back to Trent.

"So to be clear, you're not taking her back to Norfolk, right?" I said.

"No," Trent replied. "Though, you're really going to have to let that go. Norfolk is my home now and my daughter should be able to come see me."

I'd wanted to take Trent to court to keep him from seeing our child. But if I didn't know anything else, I knew he'd be a good father, and the last thing I'd ever want to do is deny a child a parent. I knew how that felt.

"She's not even two yet."

Trent sighed like he wasn't going to bother arguing with me. "Well, we are just celebrating my parents' anniversary so we'll be here all weekend. And she'll be in one piece when you get back."

I ignored his sarcasm and leaned in and kissed my daughter again.

"Bye, sweetie. Mommy loves you."

As I watched my daughter being whisked away, April came up behind me. "Funny how things have a way of working out," she said.

I nodded. I had been pregnant the whole time in Atlanta and had no idea. I felt especially disgusted when two weeks after Alex's funeral, I found out I was pregnant. Because the first thing that flashed through my mind was, *Who was the father?*

The fact that I was even in a predicament to question who I was pregnant by brought on a shame that took me months to recover from.

Thankfully, the doctor confirmed that I was nine weeks along, which meant that it was Trent's baby. He'd been ecstatic about the news.

He'd also been in a serious relationship with Symone by the time I told him.

"You ready to head to the airport?" April asked.

I nodded. I'd been back to Atlanta a few times. I was heading back this time because Sarah had invited me to Sunny's first-grade graduation. I don't know that we'd ever be where I

wanted us to be, but at least I was further down that forgiveness road. We both were.

My mother and Anthony hadn't made it. At first I felt sick
at the idea that I really had caused them to get a divorce. But
on my third visit to Atlanta to see her, she had confessed that
I hadn't been the first, and she doubted that I would've been
the last.

"I got tired of living a lie," she'd told me. I wasn't sure if
that was in reference to me or him.

Either way, I was happy that I'd sought out Sarah . . . and
found her. No, the story hadn't ended the way that I had
hoped, but Nicolette had shown me that stories don't really
end. They just start new chapters.

And I couldn't wait to see where this chapter took me.

A NOTE FROM
THE AUTHOR

I'm one of those women who love their mothers, like down to their core. My mother is my heart. Okay, maybe I wished some evil things upon her in my teen years because she was strict, but I thank her for all those things now.

Growing up, my mother was never my friend. She made that clear: she had enough friends. Her job was to be my mother. We became friends when I was grown and I always heard stories about mother-daughter relationships that were the polar opposite. And they always fascinated me. Couple that with stories I'd heard of men bailing on their children and my writer's mind got to churning.

That's how all my stories start: with a *What if?*

I thought, what if a mother decided, for whatever reason, she wasn't really cut out to be a mother? Is it really possible not to have a maternal gene? And then, what if, years later, that gene shows up?

That's where *Seeking Sarah* was born.

I wanted to explore the complexities of being a mother. Then, of course, you know I had to throw in a little drama.

But at its core, *Seeking Sarah* is a story about finding something you so desperately crave, and losing yourself in the process.

I hope you enjoyed and will tell a friend or three.

I've lost count of which book number this is. I don't know if that's a good thing or a bad thing. But I've been blessed to have a long and somewhat successful career doing what I love. I wouldn't be able to do what I love were it not for my crew:

My husband of twenty-plus years, Dr. Miron Billingsley, who as a newlywed snuck our bill money, bought me a computer, and told me, "Write." Thank you for being there every step of the way.

My three wonderful children, who keep me grounded and are not the least bit impressed with what I do and just want to know if I will "be home in time for their game." Mya, Morgan, and Myles, everything I do, I do for you.

I am the luckiest sister on earth. Tanisha Tate, I may not show it, I may not let you know it, but I am proud to call you my sister.

My business partner, writing partner, and Jill of all trades, Victoria Christopher Murray. For helping me flesh out my stories, for picking up the slack when I'm slacking, for providing motivation and encouragement . . . a thousand thank-yous.

Pat Tucker, distance may have changed the dynamics, but I am forever grateful for your support and friendship.

My core . . . my forever ride-or-die friends who whether they read the books or not continue to support me and, more importantly, be there for me no matter what: Jaimi Canady, Raquelle Lewis, Kim Wright, and Clemelia Humphrey Richardson, love you for life!

To my soror, my friend, my publicist, Norma Warren. I

know I have given you a few extra gray hairs, but you will never know how eternally grateful I am that you came into my life. I promise you, I'm working hard to #DoBetter.

To my BGB admin family: Jason, Cheritta, Princess, Kimyatta . . . thank you so much for all that you do. To our amazing partners . . . I'm so honored to be affiliated with you! We're truly changing the game!

As usual, thanks to my agent, Sara Camilli; my editor from the beginning, Brigitte Smith; my wonderful publicist, Melissa Gramstad; and the rest of my family at Gallery. Thank you for believing in me!

I also have to show major love to those who helped my movie dreams come true: D'Angela Proctor at TV One, who told me years ago she would make one of my books into a movie, and she did. *The Secret She Kept* is one of my books that is near and dear to my heart and I'm so thrilled TV One brought it to the screen. Thanks also to Karen Peterkin, Alton Smith, Rhonda Baraka, and the fabulous team that brought my words to life.

I'm one blessed author because I also have a movie currently on Netflix. *Let the Church Say Amen* would've never happened were it not for Regina King and Reina King. I will continue to be grateful to you ladies. Thanks also to Queen Latifah's Flava Unit, BET, Bobcat Films, T. D. Jakes, and all the talented actors and crew . . . for helping my dreams come true.

A thousand thanks to my friends and literary colleagues: Nina Foxx, Tiffany Warren, Renee Flagler, Eric Jerome Dickey, Lolita Files, and Curtis Bunn. Special shout-outs to: Monique S. Hall, Raine Bradley, Sharon Lucas, Yolanda

Gore, Naturopath Cecie, Sophie Sealy, Lisa Paige Jones, King Brooks, Eddie Brown, Tiffany Tyler, Michelle Chavis, Gina Johnson, Pam Gaskin, Ivy Levingston, Ruthleen Robinson, Orsayor Simmons, and my sister-cousin, Shay Smith.

I'm always skeptical about this next part, as I know there are so many book clubs that support my work. So let me just say a gigantic thanks to all of you who have supported me over the years.

Thank you to all the wonderful libraries that have also supported my books, introduced me to readers, and fought to get my books on the shelves.

To all my wonderful Facebook friends, especially the ones who comment and support on the regular: Nelvia, Tamara, Trevy, Ericka, Angela, Bernice, Davina, Michelle, Tracey, Karyn, Crystal, Nina, Eddgra, Tonia, Kimberlee, Cindy, Annette, Nicole, Chenoa, Brenda, JE, Tanisha, Beverly, Dwon, Noelle, LaChelle, Kim, Princis, Joe, Charlenette, Karla, Yasmin, Terri, Tres, April, Cheryl, Kelley, Katharyn, Tashmir, Bridget, Juda, Alicia, Arnesha, Tamou, Antoinette, Cynthia, Jackie, Ernest, Wanda, Patrick, Lissha, Tameka, Laura, Marsha, Wanda, Kym, Allison, Jacole, Stephanie, Dawn, Paula, Nakia, Jodi, Cecily, Leslie, Gary, Cryssy, KP, Tomaiya, Gwen, Nik, Martha, Joyce, Yolanda, Lasheera. (Y'all know I could go on and on . . .) Here's a giant virtual hug!

Lots of love and gratitude to my sorors of Alpha Kappa Alpha Sorority Inc. (including my own chapter, Mu Kappa Omega), my sisters in Greekdom, Delta Sigma Theta Sorority Inc., who constantly show me love . . . and my fellow mothers in Jack and Jill of America (particularly, the Durham chapter, led by the fabulous Makeba McDaniel).

And finally thanks to you . . . my beloved reader. If it's

your first time picking up one of my books, I truly hope you enjoy. If you're coming back, words cannot even begin to express how eternally grateful I am for your support. From the bottom of my heart, thank you!

Much Love,
ReShonda

SEEKING
SARAH

ReShonda Tate Billingsley

This readers group guide for Seeking Sarah *includes an introduction, discussion questions, and ideas for enhancing your book club. The suggested questions are intended to help your reading group find new and interesting angles and topics for your discussion. We hope that these ideas will enrich your conversation and increase your enjoyment of the book.*

INTRODUCTION

Brooke Green has been motherless since she was seven years old. Growing up with her loving father, a piece of Brooke had always felt missing, lost long ago on the day of her mother's death. Now, in her midthirties, Brooke finds herself drowning in grief after her father succumbs to a stroke. But in the wake of losing a parent, Brooke shockingly regains another when she learns a startling truth that changes her life forever: her mother, Sarah, is very much alive. At her father's funeral, Brooke's grandmother reveals that Sarah had walked out on her family amid claims that she wasn't fit for motherhood; her father lied about Sarah's death in an attempt to protect Brooke. In search of more details, Brooke hires a PI to track Sarah down and discovers that her mother is now working as an elementary school principal in Atlanta, and happily raising another daughter. Stunned, Brooke is torn between her desire for answers and her thirst for revenge against the mother who abandoned her. Bestselling author ReShonda Tate Billingsley delves into the complicated, emotional, and often painful mother-daughter bond in her gripping novel *Seeking Sarah*.

TOPICS AND QUESTIONS
FOR DISCUSSION

....

1. When we first meet Brooke, we learn that she has already lost both a mother and a fiancé, leaving her convinced that, when it comes to love, "forever didn't exist" (p. 2). Discuss the character of Brooke in these early scenes: a woman who's both emotionally hardened and emotionally vulnerable. Do you relate to her, and in what way?

2. Brooke wears two rings around her neck: her mother's wedding ring, and her engagement ring from Jared. What symbols or mementos do you wear, carry with you, or display in your home that represent people you love?

3. Brooke's flashbacks consistently return her to emotionally painful moments featuring her mother—those instances of turmoil seem to be her most distilled memories. Why do you think these are the memories that begin resurfacing for Brooke? On a narrative level, how do these scenes hint at the reasons behind Sarah's decision to flee?

4. Brooke struggles to wrap her mind around the truth about her mother, thinking: "I had heard stories of back in the day, fathers who went to the store for bread and never returned. But this, a mother abandoning a child? That was insane. Mothers don't abandon their children" (p. 47). In what way would this story be different if it were a father-daughter story rather than a mother-daughter story? Why does a mother's abandonment cut so much deeper?

5. One of the tensest scenes from the first act of the novel is Brooke's dinner with Trent, when she tells him about the private investigator (and the accompanying price tag). Trent is obviously affected by this decision. What was your reaction to this scene? Do you think his reaction was justified? Explain your reasoning.

6. When Brooke finds out her mother's name and location, what did you anticipate would happen next? What action did you envision her taking? What action would you have taken if you were Brooke, armed with that information?

7. Brooke is heartbroken upon realizing that, in her words, "the man I loved was the biggest obstacle to reuniting with my mother" (p. 100). Do you sympathize with Trent's refusal to support Brooke's move to Atlanta? Why or why not?

8. Brooke learns that Sarah Ford now works as an elementary school principal—does that job title surprise you?

9. Identify and discuss the moment (or moments) when Brooke's desire to get to know her mother transforms into a thirst for revenge instead. Do you relate to that delicate balance between sadness and anger that Brooke is grappling with?

10. As Brooke spends more time in Atlanta, she fully inhabits three different identities: Mona, Meredith, and Brooke. As tension mounts, Brooke thinks, "I felt like I was swimming in a cesspool of lies" (p. 182). Do these lies create a protective shield that empowers Brooke to take bold action, or is she losing her "true self" in this web of lies?

11. Describe your reaction to Brooke's decision to seduce her mother's husband. In your opinion, does she take her revenge mission too far?

12. On page 242, Nina's assistant, Amiya, comments, "Revenge is a confession of pain." Even though Amiya is trying to talk sense into her boss, the statement resonates with Brooke. How could these wise words reframe the way you view Brooke's actions against her mother?

13. Before the novel's dramatic climax, was there a moment when you sensed that Alex could be dangerous? If so, describe the scene or interaction that first revealed another side of this troubled character.

14. Increasingly complicated dynamics play out among Brooke, Sarah, Anthony, Alex, and Trent in this novel,

especially in the final chapters. Ultimately, who do you see as the novel's "villain," if anyone?

15. The novel ends on a note of hope, as Brooke is embarking on her own motherhood journey. How do you think the experiences of the novel will shape Brooke and inform her decisions as a mother?

16. In her "Note from the Author," ReShonda Tate Billingsley explains that "at its core, *Seeking Sarah* is a story about finding something you so desperately crave, and losing yourself in the process" (p. 276). In what way does Brooke lose herself, and, in your opinion, does she ultimately find herself again?

ENHANCE YOUR
BOOK CLUB

1. This novel predominantly takes place in Atlanta, Georgia. In honor of the book's setting, serve up cocktails that capture the flavor of the Peach State, such as peach sangria or a peach Bellini. You can make a peach Bellini by simply combining frozen peaches with your preferred sparkling white wine, plus a splash of peach schnapps and some ice. Blend your concoction before serving!

2. Tyler Perry's 2007 film *Daddy's Little Girls* explores similar themes to those in *Seeking Sarah*. Host a screening of the movie, which stars Idris Elba and Gabrielle Union, before your book club meeting. Discuss how the depiction of the mother in this film compares with ReShonda Tate Billingsley's complicated take on motherhood.

3. Brooke revisits the pain of growing up motherless by reading old letters that she wrote to Sarah, describing the struggles of her adolescence. Ask each member of your book club to bring an old letter, journal, diary en-

try, or even social media post to your discussion. Share these snapshots of your youth—whether painful or humorous—and discuss how your mother (or a mother figure) helped you navigate the issue or situation in question.

4. The first book that Alex recommends to Brooke is *Child of God* by Lolita Files, which tells the story of a Southern family torn apart by the secrets it struggles to keep. Read this novel in conjunction with *Seeking Sarah*, and compare and contrast the complex family dynamics portrayed in both books.